We danced in
Bloomsbury Square

We danced in Bloomsbury Square

JEAN ESTORIL

Illustrated by Muriel Wood

Follett Publishing Company
Chicago

Copyright © 1967 by Jean Estoril.
First published 1967 by William Heinemann Ltd., London.

Published 1970 in the United States of America by
Follett Publishing Company. All rights reserved.
No portion of this book may be reproduced in any form
without written permission from the publisher. Manu-
factured in the United States of America.

ISBN 0-695-40083-5 titan binding
ISBN 0-695-80083-3 trade binding

Library of Congress Catalog Card Number: 78-88865

First Printing E

CONTENTS

The Exciting Suggestion

Debbie and I started to learn ballet soon after our eighth birthday. This happened because we went to see the Royal Ballet Company when they were dancing at the Royal Court Theatre in Liverpool. *Les Sylphides*, the second act of *Swan Lake* and *Façade* were on the programme, but this meant nothing at all to us until the curtain actually went up.

Ours was not the kind of family that went often to the theatre. In fact, until then I think that Debbie and I had only been to the Christmas pantomime. The theatre just wasn't in our scheme of things, though I know now that, to many people, going to plays, opera and ballet is an essential part of life, almost as much taken for granted as eating and sleeping.

Mother took us to see the Royal Ballet that night because our next door neighbour was taking her twelve-year-old daughter. Barbara learned dancing at a school in Liverpool, and Mrs Brown said to Mother that she thought we were old enough to start taking an interest. Mother has told us since that she was really quite convinced that we'd all be bored. She thought that *she* would be, and she believed that we would wriggle and ask to be taken home before the performance was half over.

Anyway, she bought three tickets for the circle. Dad said why not do the thing properly and pointed out that if we sat at the back in cheap seats we might get someone huge in front of us and then we'd have no view at all. So our seats were in the front row of the circle; very grand.

I don't think I shall ever forget one single thing about that evening, though it is already a long time ago, and Debbie says she won't forget either. From the moment when we took our places in the warm, lighted theatre neither of us said a word. We leaned on the rail in front of us and stared down into the stalls, watching the people arrive, including a great many children who looked as though they all learned ballet. Then the members of the orchestra settled themselves and began to tune up, and presently the theatre darkened.

Since then I have been to many, many performances of ballet, often even to the Royal Opera House, Covent Garden, but that was the very first time. I remember now exactly how I felt when the curtain went up and I saw those grouped, white-clad figures in the dim light. And when they began to dance . . . well, it was like fairyland, and heaven—something quite out of this world. I don't remember even breathing for a very long time, but I do remember that during the mazurka Debbie slid her hand into mine and we held on to each other tightly.

Then, when the interval came, and the lights went up and people began to talk and offer each other chocolates, Debbie gave a huge sigh and said:

'I'm going to learn how to dance like that.'

She only just beat me to it. The words were trembling on my own tongue.

'Don't be silly, Debbie!' Mother said. 'You couldn't! A little girl of eight.'

'Barbara says she wants to be a dancer,' I pointed out. 'Why shouldn't we learn, too?'

Mother looked from Debbie to me.

'I don't know much about it, but it takes many years of training to dance like that, Dorrie. It's hard work.'

'We don't mind,' I said. 'We *will* work.'

I remember saying that, but of course I didn't understand in the least just how hard the work would be. Yet some part of my mind fully realised that those fairylike forms had been *people* and that what they could do might some day be achieved by Deborah and Doria Darke.

The second act of *Swan Lake* was another wonderful experience, but I think we were both startled by the last ballet, which was so very different. There is nothing dreamlike about *Façade*, but after a while we got the idea and even laughed. It really was funny to see dancers pretending to milk a cow, and it was all so gay.

3

We talked about what we had seen all the way home; on the bus that took us down to the Pier Head and then on the ferry-boat that took us across the River Mersey to Birkenhead. It was October then and cold on the river at night, so we had to go inside and not walk round the top deck, which we both liked far better.

By the time we reached home Mother must have known that she was beaten, for she said to Dad, who had turned off the television to listen to our story:

'These two have decided that they're going to be ballet dancers. They want to go to that place where Barbara has her classes. The Grayland School of Dance.'

They exchanged glances and I remember that my heart leaped with anxiety, because ballet lessons would cost money and, in spite of seats in the circle, we were not well off. At that time and for some years afterwards Dad managed a radio and television shop in Birkenhead.

'Maybe they'll have forgotten all about it by Monday,' Mother added, as a kind of aside, and went upstairs to make sure that our baby brother, Bim, was all right.

But we didn't forget and by the next Friday, after school, we were being interviewed by Miss Grayland at her dancing school in Mount Pleasant, Liverpool. The result was that we were going to have one ballet lesson a week. Debbie, who is much less shy than I am, was just the same then and she turned down all suggestions that we might just learn tap or modern dancing. It had to be ballet or nothing.

By the time we were eleven, and at a Grammar School in Birkenhead, we were attending two ballet classes a week at the Grayland and had passed some of our exams. We always had good roles when the Grayland put on a show, too, and Miss Grayland occasionally said that it was a pity we were not identical twins, because the audience would have found that very fascinating.

But we are *not* identical. Debbie is very fair, her hair is almost silvery in some lights, and her eyes are blue. I am much darker in every way and have hazel eyes. We are not alike in character, either, for Debbie gets on much better with people, being a much more cheerful and casual kind of girl. She wasn't casual about her dancing, though; she always worked hard. Miss Grayland never said anything to make me aware of it, but by the time we were twelve I was beginning to realise—with much secret pain— that she was a better dancer than me. I had mistakes of posture that were very hard to correct; Debbie had the perfect body for a ballet dancer. I had a little trouble with my feet; Debbie never did. She got higher marks in the exams as well.

We never spoke of this to each other, and as a matter of fact I was one of the best dancers in the class. It was just that Debbie was outstanding. I hated myself for being jealous, but in my heart I would have given anything in the world to be like my twin, down to the last shining strand of hair and perfectly shaped bone.

As the years passed we saw a great many professional ballet companies, for we were lucky enough to live near a city that usually gets several visits a year. We had learned a tremendous lot by watching the Festival Ballet, the Ballet Rambert, and of course the Royal Ballet. We had seen the Lingeraux Company as well, and Cécile Barreux was one of our favourite ballerinas. We also read all the books about ballet that we could lay hands on, and were always given them for our birthday. By then Dad and Mother were quite resigned, even proud of us, but Dad sometimes said he didn't know where on earth it would lead. He didn't think the life of a ballet dancer any sort of a life at all and never missed an opportunity to point out that we'd do better to concentrate on our ordinary lessons and perhaps be teachers or something.

'Perhaps they'll join the Television Toppers or some other famous team,' Mother once said hopefully. 'There *must* be money in that.'

'Or we could put on our own act,' Debbie said facetiously. 'You know, the Darke Sisters.'

'The Darke Dancers, would be better,' I added, knowing of course that she wasn't serious, though Dad looked as though he thought it a good idea, if we had to dance at all. I knew that we didn't particularly want money. We only wanted to struggle on towards our goal of being real ballet dancers, hard work, provincial digs and all.

Anyway, I had to give you our background, but this story really starts in early September, just before our thirteenth birthday. By then Barbara Brown was working in an office and had quite forgotten that she ever wanted to be a dancer. As a matter of fact she was engaged and planning to be married as soon as her parents agreed that she was old enough.

But Debbie and I sometimes told each other that we were never going to get married. Though of course lots of ballet dancers do have husbands and even children.

Well, to get back to that September day: we had just returned from our holiday in North Wales and would be back at the Grammar School in a couple of days. The Grayland had been closed during the holidays, but classes were just starting again and we were excited at the thought of dancing again. We always tried to practise wherever we might be, but our house was quite a small one, with a squashy bathroom. Towel-rails are useful things for holding while one does exercises, but there really wasn't room to do much in our bathroom in Marshland Road.

It was wonderful to get off the bus near the Adelphi Hotel and to hurry up Mount Pleasant. Wonderful to run up the steps of the Grayland and along the hall, then down into the rather dreary cloakrooms. Everyone was chattering about holidays as they changed into tights and tunics and carefully tied their ballet shoes.

During the past year Miss Grayland had handed over most of the ballet classes to a Mrs Bettle, who was a very good teacher. She used to teach at the Royal Ballet School until her husband was moved to Liverpool.

So there we were back in the big studio, warming up at the *barre*, and I was very happy to be back, because those familiar exercises were the only thing in my life that seemed desperately important.

Half-way through the centre practice Miss Grayland came in and stood leaning on the piano, watching intently. Then after a few minutes she said something to Mrs Bettle and went away again. As soon as the class was over Mrs Bettle said:

'Miss Grayland wants to see the Darke twins in her office.'

Debbie and I looked at each other in a startled way, and I at once wondered if we were in some kind of trouble. But it didn't seem likely, as we hadn't been there for nearly six weeks.

'Come on, silly! Didn't you hear? We're wanted,' said Debbie. She took my hand and hauled me along to the office.

Miss Grayland was standing by the window, and when we appeared her secretary gathered up some papers and went out of the room. Miss Grayland turned round and smiled warmly at us.

'Sit down, girls. I want to talk to you, I've a suggestion to make.'

We obeyed, and Debbie squeezed my hand before she let go.

'You are both quite convinced that you want to be ballet dancers?' Miss Grayland began.

I nodded dumbly, and Debbie said:

'Oh, yes. But we don't know how we're to manage it. We ought to be having more than two classes a week now, oughtn't we?'

Miss Grayland nodded in her turn.

'It would be difficult here, even if I were to let you take extra classes free. You can't really spare the time to come to Liverpool more often after school, and it wouldn't be good for you. You'd be tired and would probably start skimping your meals or your school work. Besides, you ought to practise every day. Now listen. Mrs Bettle quite agrees with me in this. You are both promising dancers and we have great hopes of you. The Lingeraux School in London is offering five scholarships and ten paying places for January, and we'd like you to go up for an audition. It's on Saturday, September 15th, which leaves us very little time.'

Debbie's hair swung out in a silver curve as she turned to look at me, and my heart seemed to go down into my stomach and return slowly to place. London! The thing we had dreamed about without ever really believing it could come true. The Lingeraux!

9

'The Lingeraux is a very good school,' Miss Grayland was continuing. 'Fully educational, of course, so your dancing would simply be part of each day's time table. But they don't take boarders and I wouldn't suggest such a thing if I didn't know that you have an aunt living in London. Your mother mentioned her once, saying that she takes students. It seemed to me that, if you were successful, you could probably live with her.'

'Aunt Eileen,' Debbie said faintly, 'Dad's eldest sister. She has—has a big house in Bloomsbury. They're mostly University students or people who are at R.A.D.A.'

'But she might take the pair of you, I suppose? If your parents would agree, of course. It would be very convenient, as the main part of the Lingeraux School is in Bloomsbury Square. Anyway, I want you both to explain to your mother and ask her to telephone me as soon as possible. As a matter of fact I've already written to the Lingeraux and they are willing to let you both try for scholarship places.'

We rose to our feet, but of course it was Debbie who had enough presence of mind to say politely:

'Thank you very much, Miss Grayland. We'll explain to Mother. We—We'll do our best.'

'I should be sorry to lose you, but you really ought to go on now to somewhere where you can concentrate fully. And you'd enjoy London. It would be a very interesting life.' Then she looked at me.

'Dorrie, you don't say much. Would you like to try, dear?'

'More than anything in the world!' I cried, almost explosively. Then I blushed and felt silly, because she looked faintly surprised. I don't usually express my feelings.

'Well, I hope you won't be too disappointed if you aren't successful. I suppose there's no chance that one of you could accept a paying place?'

'None at all,' Debbie said positively. 'It must cost a terrible lot.'

'I'm afraid so. Then of course your parents might have to pay your aunt for your board during the term. I don't want,' she went on doubtfully, 'to upset your parents at all. And I don't want you to be too sad if it falls through. Just explain and then see what happens.'

Debbie and I walked out into Mount Pleasant. Grey old Liverpool looked better than usual in the brilliant sunshine, but I was already thinking of London, the city I had only visited twice. Of course it would mean leaving home—Dad and Mother, Bunty and little Bim—but heaps of rich girls went away to boarding-school and we would be home in the holidays.

'Oh, Debbie! Oh, Debbie! Oh, Debbie!' I cried, as we took our places in the bus queue.

'Shhh! People are staring.'

'But, Debbie, it couldn't come true!'

'It might,' said Debbie. 'I suppose there's a

chance. *If* they gave us scholarships. Though there would be fares and new clothes as well as all the rest. But somehow I *believe* it could happen. Something *has* to happen; I've known that for months. If we're ever going to be dancers at all we've got to get to London

We rattled and bumped down to the Pier Head and then raced for the boat, which was giving warning hoots. We dashed across the gangway and then up the stairs to the top deck. Almost at once the gangway went up and the ferry-boat moved out into the grey waters of the Mersey.

I looked at the familiar scene, at the towers of the Liver Building against the blue sky and the Cathedral rising on the hill in the distance, and knew that I was a different person from the Doria Darke who had crossed to Liverpool only two hours before. I had seen the chance of a wider life, with dancing every day. I wanted it so much that I thought I should die if we couldn't even go to the audition.

'You always look on the dark side,' said Debbie, as we ran for our bus on the Birkenhead side.

It was an old joke. 'Darke by name and dark by nature!' one of our teachers at school had once said to me in an irritated tone. That was one day when she couldn't understand me and I wasn't helping her much.

'But, Debbie, if we can't try—'

'We'll try,' said Debbie.

12

✳ 2 ✳

London

Marshland Road is one of those rather grim Birken-head streets with rows of almost identical houses, mostly built of red brick, with tiny gardens in front and yards behind them. But at the north end of the street there are a few semi-detached houses that are slightly bigger and slightly less ugly. We lived in one of these, No. 35. There were sooty laurel bushes at the front, but at the back there was a small garden with a rose bed and some grass. Only the grass was always rather bare because Bunty and Bim played on it so much.

But when we arrived back from Liverpool on that momentous day both the younger ones were out in the street, Bunty, who was eight then, playing ball with the children from next door, and Bim riding up and down the pavement on his shabby old tricycle.

They both shouted to us and I realised then that if the dream came true, and we *did* go to London, it was going to be awful to have to say good-bye to them and to everyone and everything familiar and dear. Bim was such a funny little boy when he was five; plump and placid and yet with an iron will. You couldn't easily make Bim do anything that didn't appeal to him.

When we went in Dad was home and was having his tea and Mother was keeping him company by drinking an extra cup of tea. We always had meals rather disjointedly on dancing days. When we were at school Debbie and I usually had a sandwich and something to drink on our way to the Grayland (we had a favourite coffee-bar near Central Station), then had our meal when we reached home.

That day Mother took one look at us and demanded:

'What's the matter, girls? Something's up, I can see that. No, wait. I'll fetch your tea first. It's sausages and chips.'

She came back with two steaming platefuls and set them before us, and I looked despairingly at Debbie. I was hungry, but I didn't think I could eat until we had told our important news.

Debbie grimaced back at me, then took up her knife and fork.

'Out with it,' Mother ordered. 'I can see that you've both got something on your minds.'

Mother is sometimes a kind of witch. She always knows. It can be very disconcerting if you are trying to keep something secret. But we weren't, that time, so Debbie explained quickly, repeating all that Miss Grayland had said. She added that we quite understood about not having much money, but if it *could* be managed —

While she talked Mother and Dad just sat looking at each other and I noticed that Mother had grown rather pale. She is like me, not Debbie, with brown hair and a good colour. But just then she wasn't as pink as usual.

When Debbie had finished there was rather a long silence, then Dad said:

'Something like this had to happen. If you're to do anything with that dancing you ought to be concentrating more. We do see that, especially after that T.V. programme you missed the other night, all about ballet training. But the first question is *would* you win scholarships?'

'We can't know till we try,' I said, speaking for the first time.

'Fair enough. But what if you fail? What's going to happen then? Won't you both be hopelessly unsettled?'

'I'm afraid we will be, anyway,' Debbie confessed. 'I mean, if we don't try at all. Miss Grayland and Mrs Bettle wouldn't recommend us to the Lingeraux if they didn't think we'd a chance.'

'And you do realise what it'd mean if you were accepted? You'd have to go two hundred miles away for three months at a time. That's supposing that Eileen would take you. Of course the whole thing would fall down if she wasn't willing. And I have the impression that you didn't like your aunt much.'

I felt myself blushing and Debbie looked rather red, too. It was two years since we had last stayed with Aunt Eileen. London had been exciting, wonderful, but even Debbie had been rather in awe of our somewhat formidable aunt.

'Dorrie was scared of her,' said Debbie unfairly.

'So were you!' I retorted, then we looked at each other and subsided. We weren't helping our case.

'We're two years older,' Debbie went on, 'We'd be thirteen and several months by January. And if she's your sister she must be all right, really.'

Dad laughed at that, a trifle ruefully.

'Eileen *is* all right. Of course she's twelve years older than me. I was the youngest of eight. I used to be a bit scared of her when I was a kid, but she means well. The trouble is that she never had any sense of humour. She's the kind who would always do more than her duty, but seemed grudging on the surface. I feel sure she'd fit you in somewhere and look after you well. In fact, she'd be sterner than we are. Not a doubt of it. Better ask your mum what she thinks.'

We turned to Mother, who said slowly:

'I'm sure I don't know what to say. I don't want to lose them, but I don't want to stand in their way.'

'I wish London was nearer,' I said, with a sigh. Two hundred miles seemed a very long way in those days.

'You'd be homesick. And it wouldn't be any good shouting that you didn't like it once you'd taken a step like that.'

'We aren't babies,' Debbie said, with dignity. 'Of course we'd be homesick, but we'd put up with it because it's the only way to get on with our dancing. Only what about the money? If everybody's going to be ruined because of us—'

Dad had been looking very serious.

'There's a bit put by, you know. I got that two hundred pounds when my great aunt died and I've saved another hundred or so. I was meaning to use some of it on you children as you needed it.'

'If we won scholarships we might get grants for uniforms and books,' Debbie remarked.

So, in the end, it was decided that we should go and try our luck at the audition. But this was dependent on what Aunt Eileen said, and there wasn't very much time, if it all had to be arranged with Miss Grayland. So Dad took some money and went out to telephone to London from the call-box at the end of the street. Debbie and I went as well, and we stood outside the box, staring at him through the glass. It seemed very remarkable that he was about to speak to someone so far away—to Aunt Eileen in that big Bloomsbury house that I well remembered. I even remembered that the telephone had been in her private sitting-room, with another 'public' one in the hall for the students.

Dad was talking very rapidly. We could even hear a few words when the street was quiet. Then he hung up and came out, smiling.

'That'll be O.K. Eileen seems to think you're both

mad to want to be ballet dancers, but she says she thinks you'd get a wonderful education at the Lingeraux and maybe it wouldn't be wasted. She'll expect you both, and your mother, on Friday evening, September 14th, and if you're successful she'll find you a room during term. She says it may be in the attics, but she'll take you and look after you—'

'Would you have to—pay?' I asked tentatively. Suddenly money seemed a great deal more important than I had thought. I wished that we had enough not to have to worry quite so much.

Dad laughed and, with Debbie and me on either side of him, set off towards our house.

'I didn't mention it and neither did she. She knows how we're fixed. Maybe she'd let you help a bit in your spare time; shopping on Saturday mornings and that sort of thing. I know she finds it hard to get help.'

Debbie pulled a face. She doesn't like domestic things and neither do I very much. But we were used to helping at home.

'I wonder if the others are all rich?' she said to me, when we were alone in our room.

'Not all, surely? There'd be other scholarship pupils.'

'I bet plenty of them are well off, all the same. Cécile Barreux has a niece in the School. Remember we read about it in that article?'

'She might be quite poor, even if her aunt pays

for her or something. And even ballerinas don't make fortunes,' I said. 'Not like film stars.'

'No, but she appears on television. That must help a lot. I expect we'll have to do the same, to step up our basic salaries as dancers.'

'Looking ahead a bit, aren't you?' I asked and she laughed, turning a pirouette that brought her up against my bed.

'Oh, bother! I would like more space.' Debbie followed the pirouette with an arabesque and the evening sun shone full on her silvery-gold hair. 'I just *know* I'm going to get there some day. We both are.'

I wished I had her certainty. Now that we were really going to have our chance I already knew that I was scared. The people at the Grayland thought that we were good, but who knew what wonderful talent might turn up at the Lingeraux on September 15th? And Debbie was a better dancer than me. *She* never said so, no one had ever said so in plain words, but I knew.

'Maybe we'll die before the 15th,' I said. 'I don't believe it will ever happen.'

We didn't die. The days passed quickly, partly, of course, because we were back at school, with almost no time for thinking. By the time we had coped with school lessons, games, homework and our extra ballet classes there was scarcely half an hour left for dreaming or even worrying. The extra ballet classes were arranged by Miss Grayland just as soon as she knew we were going to try for scholarships, and she even coached us herself when no one else at all was there.

She explained that she didn't think we would actually have to dance. It would be a matter of exercises and a medical examination. That, she believed, was what happened at the Royal Ballet School auditions and some others. She had never actually sent any pupils to a Lingeraux audition before, but, just in case we had to dance, we were to do something simple out of the last show the Grayland had given. She made us practise one or two of the dances and provided us with music. Another thing she said was that she felt sure the Lingeraux would get a report on our school work from the Grammar School. This I found alarming news, though Debbie looked complacent and remarked that she had been top five weeks running at the end of last term.

Debbie had rather thought that we would wear tutus for the audition, but Miss Grayland said not. We were to wear our Grayland tunics, which were blue.

All our friends were astonished that we were going to London on such an important mission and the *Birkenhead News* published a little paragraph about us, calling us 'The Ballet Twins'.

'Fine fools we shall feel if we don't do any good,' said Debbie. 'I can't think how on earth they heard.'

Debbie said she was nervous, but I didn't believe it. I was scared stiff. I'd wake up in the middle of the night and feel cold with terror, and then hot.

Sometimes, in the night, I thought of what it would be like to live in London. We would be able to go to Covent Garden on Saturday afternoons; in the Gallery, of course, if we saved up our pocket money. But, without paying a penny, we could wait at the stage door of the Opera House and see the great ones. We would be *there*, on the spot. We would walk along Piccadilly . . . see the spring come to the London parks . . . be able to go to places like the National Gallery whenever we liked.

If we failed, if the whole thing came to nothing, Liverpool would never be the same again. Our old life would be dust and ashes. We would probably never be real ballet dancers.

Then, unbelievably, we were in the train on our way to London, wearing our Grammar School uniforms, since they were quite our most respectable clothes. Debbie was a little annoyed about this, but Mother was adamant. I didn't mind what I wore; I was so churned up that I could hardly sit still. In fact I spent a lot of the time standing out in the corridor, watching the September dusk falling over the Midland fields and farms. It was all so dreamlike that I didn't feel like Dorrie Darke at all, though sometimes I wondered how we would return on Sunday. In triumph, or with the whole thing at an end?

It was nearly nine-thirty when we reached Euston

and the noise and the crowds added to the strange feeling of unreality that held me. But Aunt Eileen was real enough; there was no doubt about that. She was waiting for us at the end of the platform, a big, rather grim-looking woman in dowdy clothes. They were the kind of clothes you never really noticed; very drab and ordinary.

She kissed us all briskly, remarked that I looked pale (small wonder!) and bustled us off towards Gower Street, where she lived. We went by bus for just a few stops, since her house was at the bottom end near Bedford Square. I would have been glad to walk.

Even the Euston Road enchanted me and the red buses and people's alien voices. I caught a glimpse of University College under the moon. Then we had left the bus and were approaching Aunt Eileen's house. It was a very attractive place, with fresh black and white paint and a blue front door, and there were wrought iron railings that made tiny balconies at each window.

Aunt Eileen married quite well. That is, her husband had enough money to buy the London house, though she once said it was going cheaply after the war, when it was in bad condition owing to the bombing. They used to let rooms to students even when he was alive and doing his own job, which was something in a shipping firm. Then, when he died, Aunt Eileen carried on. Three of her children were married by then, but Linda was still at school. At the time of which I am writing Linda was eighteen and worked in an office in Red Lion Square.

Aunt Eileen led us into the hall, where I at once saw the telephone that I remembered and the letter-rack for the students. A huge street map of London was pinned on the wall nearby. She was talking briskly as she went towards her sitting-room.

'Linda's out. When is that girl ever in, anyhow? She's got over her beatnik phase, when she spent hours sitting in coffee-bars and never washed her hair. Now she's always experimenting with her appearance and is crazy on dancing. I can tell you, Frances,' to Mother, 'she's quite an anxiety to me. I shall be glad when she's safely married. She takes far too much interest in the students here.'

'Do they take an interest in her?' Mother asked, sounding faintly amused.

Aunt Eileen gave a kind of snort.

'Some do, but they have their own friends at the University or wherever they're studying. Linda's my own flesh and blood, but even I can't see that she has many brains. She's out of her depth in all their talk about the "bomb" and the state of the world. Linda's more interested in next week's pleasure than in starving children in China or what may happen to the world if we aren't careful. I hope yours are bright. I can't imagine that it takes many brains to be a ballet dancer yet they say that the education is first class at the Lingeraux.'

'Our brains are all right,' said Debbie, rather

23

pertly. 'And ballet does take intelligence, you know. It's not all muscle. You have to know about all kinds of things; music and art and—'

Mother gave her a quelling look and she grew silent. We stood in a little group on the hearth-rug, glad of the fire, because it had been chilly out. Aunt Eileen went on:

'Look! There's a cold supper ready. What would the girls like to drink? Better be milk as it's getting late. I've given you two the best room,' she said, in much the same tone she had used all along. 'Thought you'd like it, just for this weekend. In term-time it's let to a new student, a New Yorker who's coming over for a year. If you're coming to live with me it'll probably be a garret that you'll get.'

If we came to live with her! I remembered, sickeningly, that tomorrow would decide what was to happen to us. The dreariest garret would be heaven if it meant that we were pupils at the Lingeraux Ballet School.

I was very glad when we had finished supper and Debbie and I were alone in the best room. It had a single bed and a kind of couch that Aunt Eileen had made up for one of us, and it was a very nice room, with a gas fire and a little ring for boiling a kettle. There were also lots of book shelves, mostly empty, and I wondered what books the New Yorker would put on them, and what kind of work he would do at the little desk.

Mother looked in when we were in bed. Debbie

and I had tossed to see which of us should have the couch and it fell to me. I didn't mind. It was very comfortable, but I didn't think I would sleep, anyway.

'We'll go for a walk in the morning,' Mother said. 'That'll be the best thing. You aren't due at the audition until two o'clock.'

'Miss Grayland said she thought they were seeing the boys in the morning,' I said.

'Funny to be in a school with boys,' Debbie murmured, when Mother had turned out the light and gone away.

'Oh, Debbie, I don't think I shall have the courage to go, after all,' I confessed. 'To the audition, I mean.'

'We'll go,' said Debbie. '*And* do well. We've just got to.'

* 3 *

The Audition

London looked beautiful in the September sunshine. The trees in the squares were still green, but there was just a hint of coming gold and the air was mellow. Soon it would be autumn.

We took the bus to Piccadilly Circus, where Mother at once said eagerly that she would like to go into Swan and Edgar's. Mother loves big stores and we couldn't very well be selfish and make a fuss, but it was rather dreadful to have to walk through the dress department, and then look at coats, when we felt so wriggly. I knew that Debbie was tense and I felt sick. It was already nearly eleven o'clock.

It was better in St James's Park, walking beside the lake and catching glimpses of the towers of Westminster and all the big buildings in Whitehall. But in a way I should have been glad not to look at London at all, because I was so ready to love every yard of it and I longed *passionately* to be back there in January.

The Lingeraux Ballet School is in Bloomsbury

Square, only quite a short distance from Gower Street. So we returned to Aunt Eileen's for lunch and didn't have to leave until a quarter to two. I scarcely ate anything, and Debbie only made a brave try. Aunt Eileen seemed a little cross with us, but just before we left I heard her saying to Mother:

'I'm used to nerves with the students. My life is always a misery when they're taking exams. The twins will be all right when they get to the audition. It's waiting that's the trouble.'

Linda was home for lunch. She was a very glamorous girl, with her reddish hair cut in the latest style and long, vividly coloured nails. We had gathered that Aunt Eileen didn't like this much better than Linda's 'beatnik' period, when she lived in the same old sweater for weeks. But we thought she looked wonderful.

'Cheer up, kids!' Linda said to us. 'You'll be all right. Going to be future Fonteyns, I hear.'

'If we get the chance,' said Debbie. She was rather green by then and my stomach was behaving strangely. It was awful.

Yet I knew that Debbie was pretty confident. She *knew* that she was a good dancer. I wasn't nearly so sure about myself and my legs felt exactly as though they were made of cotton wool as we set off.

'I never thought,' said Mother, as we walked down Bloomsbury Street and turned into Great

Russell Street by the British Museum, 'that I'd ever be taking my twins to a London audition.'

She seemed nervous herself, which wasn't reassuring, and I gripped my little case even tighter. Very soon we reached Bloomsbury Square and there was the Lingeraux School, two big houses painted cream and black and with a board that said:

Lingeraux Ballet School for Boys and Girls
Fully Educational
Information from Madame Lingeraux or the
Headmistress

Several people were going up the steps as we approached. There was a black-haired girl of about our own age with a very pretty, stylish mother, and a little girl with a fair pony-tail who was clinging to an elderly woman's hand. It looked like her grandmother and *she* was not stylish at all. In fact, they both looked quite poor. The little girl's coat had been let down rather obviously. It was, curiously, a bit cheering.

So we walked up the steps of the Lingeraux and it was like going into the promised land, even though the entrance hall was dark and quite ordinary; shabby, really. A young woman was sitting at a table, ticking off names on a list. When it came to our turn she said:

'Oh, yes, the Darke twins from Birkenhead. Follow the others, my dears. Miss Verney is showing them where to change.'

I looked desperately at Mother, who had joined the other two adults. She looked rather lost herself.

'Everyone is waiting in the hall,' the young woman said reassuringly. 'You'll join your mothers there.'

Debbie and I went down into the cloakrooms, which were in the basement, just as they were at the Grayland. There was quite a crowd of girls of all ages, all in different stages of undress. There was something about the smell of the place that was comforting and I tried to imagine that we really were at the Grayland, just getting ready for a class. But my fingers were clumsy and fumbly and I was shivering in spite of the stuffy atmosphere.

After a few minutes, when I had managed to get into my tunic, I began to listen to scraps of conversation. A girl of about fifteen was saying loudly:

'I must say I don't think much of the *look* of the Lingeraux. Not very impressive, is it?'

'Oh, it's far bigger than it looks,' another girl assured her. 'My cousin came here. She's in the Company now. There's a hall and some studios built on at the back, and more studios in the same building as the Company rehearsal rooms just a few streets away. Then of course the Lingeraux Theatre is just off the bottom of Kingsway.'

'I *know* where the Lingeraux Theatre is,' the other one said loftily. 'Anyway, there are plenty of other ballet schools. Only my teacher at Croydon seemed to think I'd better try for the Lingeraux first. The

Company is quite a good one, though small. They do a lot of interesting experimental things.'

'I'm afraid we're pretty far from getting into the Company just at the moment.'

Another girl not much older than us was talking about Covent Garden.

'The new ballet last Saturday was marvellous. You should have heard the applause at the end and seen all the flowers. And she—Oh, she really is the most wonderful dancer in the world! I went to the stage door and got her autograph—'

'I'm going to be sick! I know I am!' a voice said frantically and I looked with sympathy at the girl nearest to me. She was brown-haired and wore a pink tunic, and, in the dim light, her face certainly looked greener than Debbie's had before we left Gower Street.

'I might be, too,' I said.

'Say we were sick right in front of *them* ... Madame Lingeraux! Fancy! Are you trying for a scholarship?'

'Yes. We can't come otherwise.'

'Neither can I. I'm Mel Forrest and I live in Campden Town. Did you say "we"?'

'Yes, my twin, Debbie. Here she is. I'm Dorrie Darke.'

Debbie finished tying her shoes and straightened herself.

'There are only five scholarship places, we were told.'

Mel Forrest groaned.

'I know. And three of them will go to boys. Will have gone already. They've seen the boys.'

Debbie and I looked at each other with dawning horror.

'Only *two*, then?'

'Well, that's what my dancing teacher said.'

'And will everyone try for them?' Debbie demanded.

'I s'pose so. Some of the better off ones will take paying places if they're offered. I can't,' said Mel sadly. 'Not a hope. My dad goes to sea and there are five of us.'

'But all these big girls . . . are *they* trying for the free places?'

'Search me! Maybe they aren't. I've heard that they prefer to take younger dancers, then they can train them in the Lingeraux way.'

'Debbie, we haven't a chance,' I whispered, as we all went up the stairs again. 'Oh, what shall we do?'

Debbie's face was set.

'We'd better pray that they all break their ankles or something!'

But no such fortunate accident was likely to happen and I felt just terrible as we were led along dim corridors and then a covered passage to a big hall. There was a stage at one end and a lot of seats scattered over the main part. The parents were sitting here and there with their daughters beside them. At first glance there seemed to be a great many girls in coloured tights and tunics. A few were wearing tutus and somehow looked unworkmanlike, out of place. Debbie whispered:

'I'm glad Miss Grayland told us. It's better to be in tunics. But, Dorrie, there are *dozens*!'

'Thirty-five,' I said, after a rapid count. 'No, thirty-six.' I felt worse than ever. Ten paying places and five scholarships, and more than half of those seemed to be going to boys.

Mother was talking to a thin, worn-looking woman with a nice face who turned out to be Mel's mother. We three sat on the edges of seats beside them, silent with fright. Every so often someone was called out or one or two new candidates appeared.

Then it got even worse, because we began to realise just what was happening as time passed. Sometimes a girl came back looking very pale, even, several times, on the verge of tears, and we heard them say to their mothers:

'We aren't to wait.'

Once or twice a girl came back looking relieved and settled down again.

It was ten thousand times worse than being in the dentist's waiting-room. It was ghastly.

It was about an hour before Mel's name was called. 'Meldreth Forrest!' She leaped up as though she had been shot and I felt sick for *her*. Yet all the time I knew that, if there really were only two scholarships, the three of us couldn't all be accepted for the Lingeraux.

The atmosphere grew more tense every minute. Hardly anyone was talking now. The girl who appeared just before Mel was called had departed in tears.

Mel came back at last. She actually had some colour in her cheeks. She sat down with a bump and said:

'I'm to wait.' She sounded as though she had been told that she would live after all, and I knew just how she felt.

Then Debbie was called. She didn't bounce up, but rose quite slowly, gracefully, tossing back her hair. Quite slowly she walked up the hall and disappeared, and somehow, watching her, I felt a queer little premonition. Deborah Darke, the famous dancer . . . the great ballerina. That would be Debbie one day. And I am ashamed to confess it, but I almost hated Debbie then, and I hated myself nearly as much for feeling like that. Debbie and I had always got on well together, though we had never been as intimate as twins sometimes seem to be. We usually had our own friends and didn't invariably do things together. Debbie had far more friends than I, for she was always popular. Occasionally I had minded very much when people said: 'Is that your *sister*? You're not alike, are you?' The surprise always seemed to mean that I wasn't as pretty or as clever as Debbie. But I had never before come near to hating her.

It was twenty minutes before Debbie came back.

33

She was still walking slowly and she held her head high. She no longer looked green, but unusually flushed. Her eyes were shining.

'I'm to wait,' she said, and then, to me: 'It's terrifying, Dorrie. Madame Lingeraux is there, and the Company ballet mistress, and the School's head of ballet. Oh, and Miss Sherwood, the headmistress, as well. All kinds of people. One is a doctor—a lady doctor. She looked at my feet and said they were perfect.'

I couldn't answer because just then *my* name was called. I don't really remember what happened after that. I must have got out of the hall somehow and into the big studio where the auditions were taking place. I remember a blur of faces and a voice saying very kindly:

'Just go to the *barre*, dear, and warm up.'

I know that I felt better when my cold fingers closed on the *barre* and gradually my stiff body relaxed. After a time one of the ballet mistresses made me do some centre practice, a quite difficult *enchaînement*. Then she said, 'Rest a minute, dear!' and they all went into a huddle, studying some papers and what seemed to be the medical certificate I had had to get from my own doctor. I kept my eyes on Madame Lingeraux. I knew her, because I had once seen her on television. She was a dumpy and rather ugly old woman with white hair, but I knew that once, long ago, she had been quite a famous dancer and later a respected choreographer.

34

I have very sharp ears, and though, they were speaking quietly, I caught a few phrases.

'Very good school report—'

'Not quite as good physique as the other one.'

The other one! Debbie, with her perfect body.

Then they asked me to sit down and the doctor examined my feet. She was very nice and tried to make me talk, but I couldn't.

After that Madame Lingeraux herself began to question me and I had to talk then. Suddenly it wasn't difficult, because she wanted to know what kind of music I liked. I told her I used to love Mozart and Beethoven and Chopin best, but that lately I was beginning to like some of the modern composers like Holst and William Walton and Malcolm Arnold.

'And do you have a record player?'

'Debbie and I are saving up for one,' I told her. 'We want one very much, only then records are dreadfully expensive. Some of them are *two pounds*.'

Madame disconcerted me by cackling with apparent amusement. She sounded rather like a witch, but looked quite good-humoured.

'I know. They are a dreadful price.' She had a very nice voice, just a trifle foreign. 'And what about concerts? You have a good orchestra in Liverpool.'

'We go with the school sometimes,' I said. I could feel my face flaming, but I felt much better.

Then she asked about art, remarking that we had the Walker Art Gallery in Liverpool and some good visiting exhibitions, and that was easy, too, because I love the French Impressionists and the Post Impressionists. I said that my favourite artists were Cézanne and Utrillo—and Degas, of course. I suppose all ballet dancers like Degas. Then I added that I loved some of the modern artists like Bernard Buffet, though I had never seen an original. Debbie and I collect postcard reproductions, when we can afford them, and I told Madame Lingeraux that as well. I found being able to talk quite a heady business, because usually I can't. It was like a miracle.

Finally they had another little consultation and then Madame said:

'All right, Doria—Dorrie, your twin called you. We've finished with you now. Will you wait, please?'

I tottered out somehow, remembering to shut the door quietly. Once outside I began to shiver again and the back of my neck ached with strain. I wouldn't have gone through that again for a hundred pounds.

After that everything goes all dim again. A long time passed, and eventually we were told that we could go down to the canteen if we liked and get some tea. By then there were not very many adults and dancers left. Most of the mothers ordered tea and seemed glad of it, but Mel and I said we couldn't eat or drink anything. Debbie ordered a cup of tea, but didn't finish it.

Nothing comes clear again until we were in a small office, alone with Madame Lingeraux . . . mother,

Debbie and me. But by then we knew that Mel had been offered a scholarship, and, unless she had been misinformed about the boys, that seemed to mean there was only one left. I felt worse than at any time that day and soon my fears were confirmed. Madame came to the point at once.

'Mrs Darke, we can offer your daughter Deborah a scholarship starting in January. This would cover her full tuition at the School and there would be a grant for uniform and books depending on your husband's income.' Debbie gave a stifled cry. 'We can also offer your other daughter a paying place. She has the makings of a very good dancer, and her school reports are satisfactory. We felt—'

I didn't hear what they felt. The room had gone dark and if I hadn't been sitting down I know I should have fallen. *Debbie* had got a scholarship and I hadn't! Dimly I heard Mother saying that she was afraid there was no hope of my taking up a paying place. That, in fact, she was afraid Debbie couldn't accept the offered scholarship because they wouldn't want her to be alone in London.

'I'm sorry, Madame, but I know my husband wouldn't agree. The girls have never been separated and—well, thirteen is very young to go away from home.' She wasn't looking at me, but her face was pale and her voice shaky.

Madame Lingeraux rose, holding out her hand.

'Well, don't decide now, Mrs Darke. Go home and consult your husband. We should be sorry to

37

lose two promising dancers. I can give you a few days in which to make up your minds.' Then she turned to me, and her hand was firm and warm. 'I'm sorry, Doria. There were only two scholarships. But I hope that somehow we'll be able to welcome both of you in January. You might try appealing to your local Education Authority, Mrs Darke. In certain cases ... but time is rather short and Education Committees can never be hurried. We have to get this whole thing settled as soon as possible. You understand that?'

Then we were outside in the dark corridor. . . . We were approaching the front door. Bloomsbury Square glowed greenly in front of us, for the door was open. We were all quite silent. I stole a look at Debbie and her lips were tight and her eyes stormy.

The full meaning of the whole dreadful business rose up and swamped me. Not only had I failed, but I was also going to ruin Debbie's chances.

'I've got to be—alone!' I gasped. 'Don't come. I'll be all right, Mother. Only let me go!'

I didn't wait to hear what she said, but rushed down the steps and turned towards Southampton Row. I was on the corner of High Holborn before I got my breath and even then my chest hurt and my eyes smarted with unshed tears.

There must be somewhere in that part of London where I could be alone to cry.

* 4 *

Dorrie's Dark Hours

I am good with maps and I had spent some time after breakfast that morning looking at the one in Aunt Eileen's hall. So, even in the midst of so much suffering, I remembered Lincoln's Inn Fields.

I got myself across the top of Kingsway and then ran along High Holborn, looking for some way through. For I thought that Lincoln's Inn Fields couldn't be far away. Very soon I found a narrow passageway and beyond it were trees and grass and some quietness.

The gardens weren't empty, by any means, on that fine Saturday afternoon, but I ran into a corner amongst some bushes and sank down on the worn grass, with my face turned away from anyone who might see. And there I cried for a long time, until I felt a little better in a weak and shaky way.

When at last I looked up there was London going on just as it had before. The big square was surrounded by tall buildings . . . the sky was blue . . . children were laughing and playing. And there was an endless roar of traffic in the distance.

But, for me, it really seemed as though life was over. Debbie had won a scholarship, but she wasn't going to be able to accept it. I don't honestly know which made me feel worse; the fact that Debbie had succeeded where I had failed, or the fact that I was going to ruin Debbie's life as well as my own. I suppose most people are selfish, so after a time I didn't care so much about Debbie, but only about my own shame and bitter, bitter disappointment. All my dreams of being a dancer were in the dust, and I did care so very much about continuing my training under proper conditions.

Of course they hadn't thought me hopeless. Far from it, when one considered the matter more calmly. They didn't offer any kind of place to all and sundry. I remembered the many stricken girls who had been told not to wait. That did help my pride a little, but it helped nothing else. I dreaded facing Mother and Aunt Eileen, but most of all I dreaded facing Debbie. I remembered her angry eyes and tight lips. Debbie had a temper, in spite of her fair, calm appearance, and I was dreadfully afraid that she would say something unforgivable.

But if I didn't go back Mother would be worried and might even call the police to look for me. So eventually I rose, dusted my skirt and began to walk slowly back towards Gower Street. Mother was on the steps when I came round the corner.

'Oh, Dorrie dear! I was so worried! Oh, Dorrie,

don't look like that! I'm sorry, dear. If we could manage it we would, but—'

'You can't h-help it,' I said. 'It's me—not being good enough.'

'There were only two scholarship places. You did wonderfully well to get a place at all. I'm proud of you both, but—'

'Debbie—' I began, and she shook her head.

'I should leave Debbie alone for a while, She's very disappointed, of course. I wish Miss Grayland had never suggested coming to London—'

Aunt Eileen didn't say much. She gave me some tea and hot buttered toast and I found that I was glad of them. The worst had happened, the uncertainty was over, and I was surprised to find that I was hungry. She said, when I had finished:

'You're the quiet one. And I always say it's the quiet deep ones who suffer most. But it's not the end of the world, girl. You'll live to look back at today and think it didn't matter very much.'

'I wish I could die!' I said. For the first time I wasn't afraid of Aunt Eileen, even though her manner was so brusque.

She snorted in rather an unladylike way.

'Everyone wishes they could die some time or other. And everyone does die, sooner or later. Life's a sad business and there's no getting away from it, so never try kidding yourself. It's only the scatter-brains like my Linda who manage to enjoy themselves for long. But you've still got your father and

mother and your sisters and brother. You've plenty
to be thankful for, though I daresay you don't see it
at the moment.'

'Debbie will hate me,' I said. We were alone during this conversation, because Mother had gone
upstairs.

'Debbie will get over it. She's disappointed,
naturally. She was rather riding her high horse, saying that she'd done better than you and why
shouldn't she come to London alone. If I'd been her
mother I'd have given her a flea in her ear. You did
well, too. The Lingeraux won't take just anyone. It's
simply a question of money, and Miss Debbie must
realise it.'

'She realises it,' I said drearily. 'Perhaps she *could*
come alone. She isn't a baby, and in any case you'd
look after her.'

It cost me a great effort to say that. I knew
that I could never bear life if Debbie had the
Lingeraux and London and I was left in Birkenhead
to the same old round of Grammar School and the
Grayland.

'Your mother won't hear of that, and I'm sure
your father won't either. Besides, twins shouldn't be
separated so young.'

'We aren't identical in any kind of way,' I said
dully. 'Sometimes I think people talk a lot of rot
about this twin business.' Which I suppose she
might have taken as rude, but she surprised me by
giving me quite a warm smile.

'You and Debbie need each other more than you know.'

I didn't see Debbie for an hour after that, then I just had to go up to our room to comb my hair and make myself look tidier. She was sitting on the bed, pretending to read, but her face was all blotchy, almost as bad as mine. We looked at each other in silence, and I went to the dressing-table and began to brush my hair.

'Where d'you go?' she asked awkwardly, after a while.

'Lincoln's Inn Fields.'

'Mum thought you'd get run over or lost.'

'I don't get lost,' I said. 'I can read m-maps.'

She got up then, flung the book down and went out of the room. She didn't mention the Lingeraux for the rest of that dreadful day or during the Sunday journey home. We had been going to catch an afternoon train, but I think we were all relieved when Mother said we'd go home in the morning. I didn't want to see any more of London, though I suppose that was silly, when it might have been my last opportunity.

The train journey was slow and rather awful. Debbie scarcely spoke and Mother pretended to read the Sunday papers. Instead of returning home in triumph we were a defeated trio, with a great bursting, unspoken problem.

It didn't remain unspoken when we got home, though. Dad had to be told what had happened and after that the battle raged. Debbie found her tongue and said over and over again that she didn't see why she shouldn't go to London alone.

'I've won the scholarship, haven't I? If you turn it down I shall never forgive you. I can't be held back by Dorrie, just because she isn't as good a dancer as I am—'

'Debbie!'

'Well, it's true. It's always been true, only no one says so. She's good, but *I'm* outstanding. Miss Grayland knows it, and Madame Lingeraux knew it, too. I—'

'You'll get a smacked bottom and go to bed at once if you go on like that!' said Dad, with rare anger.

Debbie's silvery hair flew out in a cloud.

'I don't see why for speaking the truth. I'm *sorry* that Dorrie didn't win a scholarship—well, naturally I am, since I'm paying for it, too. So—'

'*Debbie!* Stop it at once, do you hear?'

'Well, I *am* suffering because Dorrie didn't do better. Why should I be held back just because—?'

I sat huddled into the oldest armchair, the one with the broken springs and squashy, comforting arms, staring at the virago that was Debbie. In a way I understood exactly how she felt and one side of me didn't blame her. She was speaking, I was sure, nothing but the painful truth. But during the last day or two we seemed to have lost each other completely. I felt as though I didn't know her, as though we had never shared things and got on pretty well, on the whole. She so clearly wasn't thinking of me and how I felt.

'I don't want Debbie or Dorrie to go away!' Bunty wailed, and burst into tears. Bim, who had been playing with his train, immediately followed suit.

'Now you've started the children crying,' Mother said, in despair, and she dried their tears and sent them out to play for a little while before tea.

Long after we had gone to bed—in silence—I could hear the voices rising and falling below. When I knew that Debbie was asleep I crept out on to the landing and tried to listen. Very wrong of me, as I was well aware, but it was so dreadful not knowing.

'I won't hear of Debbie going alone, and that's flat!' Dad was saying, very loudly.

'I agree with you, Jack. But she'll be impossible to live with if we turn down that scholarship.'

'She's behaving badly. Even if the kid is disappointed she ought to think of others. It's Dorrie I'm sorry for. I only wish there was enough money to pay those whacking high fees, and uniform and books. What I've got saved wouldn't last long and we'd need most of that for fares and clothes and extras. It wouldn't end with uniform. They'd have to have plenty of other things, party frocks and such, and probably money for theatre tickets. No, it's no good. And I won't appeal to the Education Committee. Besides, as Madame Lingeraux said, it might take months. Let's make a decision now and write and say it's no go. I always knew this ballet business would do the girls no good.'

Then there was silence until the television sound suddenly came on loudly. It seemed to be the end of a play. I crept back into bed and presently music reached me through the floor. It was the Waltz of the Flowers from the ballet *Casse Noisette*. And at once I could see dancing figures and Little Clara sitting, smiling and eager, on her throne. It was almost unbearable.

One of them must have recognised the music, because it was suddenly switched off in the middle of a bar. I burrowed down, pulling the sheet almost over my head, and presently I fell asleep.

Four dreadful days followed. Mother had written to Madame Lingeraux to tell her that we would definitely not be joining the School in January. Debbie knew this and was white-faced and sulkily silent. She was off her food and complaining of headaches, and, by mutual consent, we avoided each other as much as possible.

It was during these days that the iron really entered into my soul. Life seemed so drab and dreary and it was awful to have to explain to our friends just what had happened. At least, I *suppose* Debbie explained to her friends. I told mine briefly that I had been offered a place, but that we couldn't afford to take it up. I hadn't many friends, anyway, but my two best ones were very sympathetic. They thought it romantic to want to be a ballet dancer. I knew, of course, that it wasn't. It's hardly romantic to want to launch yourself on years of hard work, with no certainty of a job at the end of them.

Mother wrote to Miss Grayland to explain, I think, but no mention was made of our going to ballet classes as usual, perhaps they were waiting for us to suggest it ourselves.

Fortunately Debbie and I didn't sit together in school, and we often did walk home separately. The worst times were in the morning and at night, when we were alone together in our room. By then I couldn't have spoken about the affair to her if my life had depended on it; my tongue felt entirely locked. I had ruined her life and mine as well. It went too deep for any words between us, though sometimes I would have given anything in the world for her to say something warm and kind, to show that we were still friends as well as twins.

By Friday I was wondering how I was going to bear it. We got up as usual and washed and dressed almost without speaking. We only made a few of the jerky, unnatural remarks that passed for conversation with us then. We went downstairs one behind the other and there was a smell of bacon and toast. Mother was just settling Bim in his place and taking the top off his boiled egg. Dad was reading a letter.

Suddenly he looked up. His face looked quite different from the strained appearance it had had since Sunday. He said, looking from Debbie to me:

47

'This is a letter from Madame Lingeraux.'

Debbie sent a plate flying off the table. It fell with a crash and broke. I stood frozen to the spot, with my plate of bacon burning my hand.

'You girls can relax. I suppose you'll be happy now. She offers Dorrie a scholarship, too.'

'It isn't true!' I cried. The smell of hot fat was making me feel sick. Somehow I managed to put the plate down on the table.

'True enough. It's a very nice letter. She says they've just learned that one of the present scholarship students is leaving at Christmas. Her family is emigrating to Australia. So Dorrie is offered the place.'

Debbie's face had flamed scarlet. She said, very shrilly:

'I always knew they wouldn't risk losing me. They wanted me—I know they did! So they'll take Dorrie as well.'

Dad put down the letter and stared at her, and Debbie seemed to realise what she had said. She began to dither.

'Well, but that's what it must be. Because you said neither of us could go—'

'Dorrie,' Dad said slowly and clearly, 'has been offered this scholarship because she deserves it, because they want *her*. I'm ashamed of you, Debbie.'

'Anyway, it's wonderful! So we can go, after all? Oh, Dorrie, aren't you thrilled?'

I was stunned. The nightmare misery of the last

few days had dropped away from me, though I knew that I would remember Debbie's words for a long time. Dad was probably right, and I had been next on the list for a scholarship, but I thought that there was always going to be a doubt in my mind. *Did* they want Debbie so much that they were willing to take me, too?

'Debbie ought to apologise to Dorrie,' said Mother. 'Really, Debbie, I don't know what's come over you lately. You want taking down a peg or two, seems to me.'

And then Debbie became much more her old self. She flung her arms round me and hugged me.

'I don't know what I said, but sorry, anyway, Dor. Who cares which of us they want, as long as we can both go? Oh, I'm so happy! So happy!'

'Well, get on with your breakfast, or you'll be late for school,' Dad said repressively.

'But aren't *you* happy, Dorrie?'

'Yes,' I said. And I *was*, because now I needn't feel guilty or ashamed, and I was going to have London and the Lingeraux.

But that week of pain and fear and misery had taught me a lot, about myself and about Debbie. I thought it would be a long time before we were really friendly again. I felt a thousand miles away from her, my 'ballet twin'.

* 5 *

A Garret in Gower Street

We settled down to our last term at the Grammar School. . . . We went back to the Grayland. Miss Grayland and Mrs Bettle were delighted with the pair of us. *Two* scholarships to the Lingeraux! We were going to be a wonderful advertisement for her dancing school.

On the surface Debbie and I went back to our old relationship, but underneath everything was quite different. I wasn't sure if she knew; if she did she made no sign. But neither of us ever once referred to that nightmare week-end in London. Only the memory of it was with me off and on, sometimes when I was walking home from school alone, or in bed at night.

It wasn't only the week-end, either; it was those dreadful days that had followed it. Scraps of conversation kept on coming back to me. 'We can offer your daughter Deborah a scholarship—' 'I can't be held back by Dorrie!' 'I always knew they wouldn't risk losing me.'

Though my dream was coming true and I was going to London to the famous Lingeraux School I seemed to have forgotten how to be happy. I knew then, more clearly than ever before, that I had always played second fiddle to Debbie. She was the prettier, the more confident, the better dancer.

I didn't always hate Debbie, of course. Even after all that had happened there were times when she won me over, made me laugh. She could be very droll and a very good companion. But all the memories were there, turning my pleasure sour. And there were times when I fully believed that the Lingeraux was taking me because it was the only way to get their future ballerina, Deborah Darke.

It was all the worse because I couldn't confide in anyone. How *could* I tell anyone in the world that I was jealous of Debbie? But it wasn't only that I was jealous; I was deeply hurt. It was as though one of the foundations of life had been removed when Debbie showed her true colours and didn't seem to like me at all. She had been upset, she had thought she was losing her big chance, but she ought to have remembered that I had feelings—so many feelings.

I tried to forget by working harder than ever before in school. I worked so hard that I even had higher marks than Debbie two weeks running. Miss Cross, our form mistress, once asked me to stay behind after school and said to me:

'I always knew you had brains, Dorrie. I wish we

weren't losing you. But what's been the matter lately? Is anything worrying you?'

'Nothing, Miss Cross,' I answered, looking at her blankly, and she sighed and said: 'Oh well, run along then.' She was the one who, in our first year, had said 'Darke by name and dark by nature.'

I worked hard at the Grayland, too, though Miss Grayland had decided, with regret, that we ought not to take part in the Christmas Show. She said we had enough to think about and what mattered was making all the progress we could before we had to face the stiff competition at the Lingeraux.

So, one way and another, the time passed quickly. November was grey and cold, with icy winds sweeping across the Pier Head. Eventually it grew so cold that we travelled to Liverpool by Underground instead of by boat, though the train cost more.

Then it was December, the big stores were gaily decorated for Christmas, the lights went on in the Birkenhead and Liverpool streets and there were brilliant Christmas trees here and there.

So that was one more thing to think about and plan for; we had all our presents to buy, never an easy business, as our pocket money didn't go very far. It took a lot of ingenuity and foresight.

By then our measurements had been sent to the big London store that made the Lingeraux uniform, but Mother said that everything else could be left until after Christmas. The new term didn't start until January 15th; it was a little later than usual because some alterations were being made at the Lingeraux and some of the studios were being painted.

Father's Christmas presents to us were both the same, lovely little blue cases for our ballet shoes and towels and things. They had silk linings and mirrors in the lids. Mother gave us each a plastic shoulder-bag in the same colour. They had safe zip pockets for money and railway tickets and other things that mustn't be lost.

Linda sent us a Christmas card—the lurid kind, simply smothered with holly and reindeers. I wished that someone would send me the kind with art reproductions on, but there is no doubt that they are the most expensive. Anyway, it was nice of Linda, and she added a message: 'Looking forward to seeing both you kids again.'

Aunt Eileen sent us plain white handkerchiefs. Her presents were always dull and useful, and now I had met her again I understood that she wasn't the kind who would ever send something pretty and use-less. But she was nice really. . . . My mind at once shied away from that bitter Saturday afternoon when she had been brusquely understanding.

Christmas was fun, mainly because Bunty and Bim were so thrilled with everything. On Boxing Day we all went to the pantomime (in quite cheap seats) and there was some rather awful ballet, but I enjoyed it all the same. I don't think I shall ever get over the breathless moment of expectation before the curtain rises.

Then our journey to London was not much more than two weeks away. I was excited and scared in about equal proportions during the first week, and then just plain scared. If Debbie was frightened she didn't say so. She was talking a lot about the Lingeraux now. Once I asked: 'Won't you be homesick?' and she was quiet for a few moments, with her head on one side. Then she said:

'Of course. I'm bound to be. I shall hate leaving them all, but we've got to, haven't we? We might have been at boarding-school for years.'

I was homesick even before I ever left. I found myself wanting to touch things like the old armchair. Yet London did beckon. I borrowed some books about it from the library and even bought a street map of my own and studied it often. I didn't want to be a country cousin; I meant to know my way about. There was a London Tube map in the new diary that Bunty had given me and I used to recite the stations on the different lines. Euston . . . Warren Street . . . Goodge Street . . . Tottenham Court Road . . . Leicester Square.

Our uniforms came in vast, impressive-looking boxes. The Lingeraux colours were grey and royal blue and there was a coat, grey with a vivid blue lining, a grey pleated skirt and a neat little jacket, several royal blue blouses and a sweater in the same colour. There was also a dark blue raincoat, a royal blue beret with a silver badge, a big, fluffy scarf and also, of course, our dancing tunics, two each. Almost everything fitted us perfectly, which Mother said was a relief. We had never had so many new clothes before and were rather overwhelmed. Even when we went to the Grammar School we got things quite gradually, starting off with a gym tunic, a blazer and a beret.

Then our shabby cases were packed and it was our last night at home. Mother had a private talk with us, telling us that she trusted us to be sensible and not cause Aunt Eileen any anxiety. We were to write as often as we could manage, at least once a week, and if we needed anything important we weren't to hesitate to explain.

'Look after each other,' she ended.

But I think I knew then that our ways were going to diverge. Debbie was all set to have a wonderful time, with hordes of new friends. I imagined myself exploring London, most probably alone. Though just occasionally I thought of Mel Forrest, who had seemed so nice. I remembered her round face and her smooth brown hair and the sound of her attractive Cockney voice. Mel was my only hope, for I expected to be very shy during the first few weeks at the Lingeraux.

So we went to sleep in our familiar beds and the next morning Mother saw us off on the London train.

The house in Gower Street seemed quite different when we arrived there on the afternoon of January

14th. There were letters in the rack in the hall, a pile of medical books spilling off the table by the front door, someone playing a radio very loudly near the top of the stairs.

Aunt Eileen, who had met us at the station, straightened the books.

'That's James MacDonald! He always leaves his books about. Still, I've got a warm spot for James. He comes from the Hebrides; his people are crofters. He's one of those hard-working Scots; a decent, serious young man. Or as serious as medical students ever are. That'll be Arthur Moorhead playing his radio so loudly. He says it helps him to study. The times I've told him it doesn't help *me* or anyone else. Of course a lot of their courses haven't started again yet, but they're all here. Most of them say they can work here better than at home. Good heavens, Sara! I thought it was an avalanche!' For, while she was talking and shutting the front door behind us, a girl had come rushing down the stairs. She wore jeans and a dirty fawn duffle coat and her hair was bright red.

'Sorry, Mrs Troom! I'm late.' The front door opened again and then slammed.

'When isn't she late? If she ever gets a real part she'll miss all her entrances. She's at R.A.D.A. Well, come along. I'll take you up. At the top, as I warned you, but your legs are young enough to stand it. You'll have Sara next door and Rachel at the end of the passage. Rachel's one of our future scientists.

Very much future just now,' she said grimly. 'I suppose she has brains, but she's the untidiest girl I've ever had here.'

She was beginning to pant a little as we toiled up three flights of stairs. She had insisted on carrying one of our cases.

'You'll soon get to know them all by sight. There's a Jamaican; a very nice, respectable boy. I don't object to coloured students. I wouldn't be so un-Christian. They have their way to make just like anyone else. There's Maribel Brown who's taking a commercial course and of course the New Yorker who has the room you were in, Clyde Smith. He seems very pleasant; plenty of money, anyone can see. It's a nice change. Well, here you are. No. 8.'

By then Debbie and I were puffing nearly as much as Aunt Eileen, for our luggage was heavy. The room was small and rather bare, with a sloping ceiling, and the window looked down into Gower Street. I saw the top of a bus as I went to the window. It was very cold, for it had snowed a little the night before. I began to shiver, but it was nice to glimpse Bedford Square touched with white, and the black patterns of the trees.

'I've put some money in your gas fire,' Aunt Eileen said, 'but do use it sparingly, please, girls. Gas just eats money these days. And always remember to turn it off when you go out of the room. I hope you'll be comfortable. It isn't luxury, but you'll make it more homelike when you've put out your things.'

'It's lovely!' Debbie said, with commendable enthusiasm. 'Book shelves, and a desk and a reading-lamp. We can do our homework up here.'

'The reading-lamp doesn't always work. I had to bring it out of Sara's room. She needs a good light. You'll do your homework down in my sitting-room while it's winter. In summer it may be different. Now get yourselves unpacked and take off those good uniforms and come down for something to eat. I provide supper for the students who want it at about seven o'clock and that's a busy time. You'll be able to help me when you settle down. I've got a woman in the kitchen mornings and evenings, and another one who comes in to clean the rooms, but I can always do with extra pairs of hands. Linda might as well not have hands at all for all the good they are.' Then she nodded and went away.

Debbie made straight for the box of matches on the narrow mantelpiece and lit the gas-fire. It popped a couple of times and then began to glow brightly. After that she bounced on each low bed in turn.

'Hard as iron. I s'pose it will be good for our spines. I don't like the colour scheme, do you?'

I stood still in the middle of the room, staring round me and shivering. The walls hadn't been papered for a long time, but you could see that there had once been pink flowers and blue bows. The curtains were what Mother calls 'dunducketty-mud' and the coverlets on the beds were not much brighter. There was a worn grey-brown carpet on the floor. It was clearly far from being the best room; it probably came just within the means of a very poor student, but then we weren't paying at all. 'It's awfully depressing,' I said, finally. 'Ours at h-home is shabby, but—but gayer than this.' But then I saw the top of another bus and caught another glimpse of a corner of Bedford Square. It was a room in London and suddenly—though I was cold, homesick and rather frightened—it had a kind of romance.

'Well, let's cheer it up,' said Debbie, beginning to struggle with her bigger case. 'Do you think Aunt Eileen will mind if we stick some of our postcard reproductions on the walls with bits of Sellotape! It couldn't do any harm.'

'Better wait until we've asked her,' I answered nervously.

Debbie found an old skirt and sweater and then divested herself with obvious reluctance of her Lingeraux uniform.

'I hope she doesn't expect us to help too much. Do you think she regards us as free labour? Because we're going to have quite enough to do, what with school and homework and amusing ourselves.'

'She's taken us for nothing,' I said, and she began to dance wildly in her vest and inelegant winter knickers, ending by flinging herself flat on her back on her bed. What springs there were creaked protestingly.

'Well, she *is* our aunt,' she said, from that position, and began flexing her ankles and toes. 'Oh, Dorrie, I do wish we were rich! I never cared much about money until lately, but now I can see just how much it matters. But at least this will sound well when I come to write my autobiography.'

'*Are* you going to write it?' I asked, scrambling hastily into the warmest sweater I could find. In spite of the gas-fire the room still seemed terribly cold. Or perhaps it was my low spirits that were making me shiver.

'We-ell, one day. Heaps of ballerinas do. Partly because they want to, I s'pose, and partly because it brings in more money. I shall start by saying, "I came to London when I was thirteen and took up residence in a garret in Gower Street. My parents were poor but honest, and—" '

Suddenly I could stand it no longer.

'You aren't a ballerina yet, and you may never be. We may both never get any further than the *corps de ballet*, or not even that far. And if you don't hurry we won't get any tea.' I knew that my voice was sharp, but I didn't care. Debbie never used to have so many airs and graces and if she ever started an autobiography at all it ought to begin: 'My twin and I came to London when we were thirteen—'

After that we got ready and unpacked almost in silence, and then, remembering to turn off the gas-fire, started off down the flights of stairs.

We were in London and tomorrow would see us both at the Lingeraux Ballet School. But just then the biggest part of me would have been glad to be safely at home.

6

First Day at Ballet School

It was already growing dark as we went slowly down the rather bleak flights of stairs, but away from the top floor it wasn't so cold. We soon realised that there was some central heating in the house, never very effective really, and not at all effective up in our garret.

Arthur Moorhead's radio was going full blast when we reached the first floor, but all the doors were closed. I wondered if the New Yorker were in and what he thought of London. It was rather peculiar to be in a house full of strangers.

Debbie boldly turned on lights as we went and when we reached the hall there was Aunt Eileen, apparently waiting for us. She gave us a little lecture on always turning lights *off* whenever possible.

'My electricity bills are just terrible. I nearly have a heart attack every time one comes in. But leave the hall light on now. I always tell myself I'd get blamed if anyone broke their neck. That's right. Now come in and make yourselves at home. I've got you a high tea ready now, as I suppose you only had sandwiches on the train.'

Aunt Eileen's sitting-room looked quite cheerful, and there was a small ginger kitten pretending to be a tea cosy on the rug; all hunched up and fluffy. The sight of it cheered me far more than the smell of cooking. I wasn't hungry in spite of the sandwiches. I fell on my knees by the kitten, for I adore cats. I think they are almost always beautiful, whatever they are doing.

'More work!' said Aunt Eileen, with a sigh, nodding at the kitten. 'It was going to be put down, so I said I'd take it. I suppose it'll keep the mice away, though all it does at the moment is play and sleep. And eat, of course. Eats its head off.'

I was growing a little used to her gloom and somehow sensed that, in spite of the grumbling tone, she rather liked the kitten.

'What's his name?'

'Ruari. James MacDonald christened it. He says it means red or something.'

The kitten rolled over, displaying a delicious stomach and a white powder-puff of a chest.

'Get your tea,' said Aunt Eileen brusquely. 'What's that you're reading?' to Debbie, who had come down with a ballet book under her arm.

'A life of Margot Fonteyn. I got it for my birthday and I've read it three times already.'

'I suppose you think of nothing but ballet. It's not a thing I understand. Lot of silly posing. The men look just ridiculous, in my view.'

'But have you seen much ballet?' Debbie asked—

rather pertly, I thought. Aunt Eileen evidently thought so, too, for she answered tartly:

'All I want to, so don't think you're going to teach me anything, Miss. I can't think where the pair of you get it from. There's never been anyone artistic on our side of the family, and I shouldn't imagine there's anyone on your mother's side.'

'We must be changelings,' said Debbie, unabashed, and she began to eat heartily.

Linda came in when Debbie and I were washing up our dishes. She brought a wonderful touch of glamour into the rather drab scullery. High boots were fashionable that winter, and hers were scarlet and shiny. She wore a black coat and a scarlet hat, very dashing, and a great deal of vivid lipstick.

'Puts all her money on her back,' Aunt Eileen said disapprovingly, and Linda laughed.

'Where else should I put it? You must admit it works.'

'You might put some into your post office savings account for a rainy day.'

'Perhaps there won't be any rainy ones,' said Linda. 'But I sometimes think I might save a bit towards my wedding.'

Aunt Eileen grunted. Linda wasn't even engaged, though we soon learned that there were three or four young men very anxious to take her out. It seemed funny that such a gloomy woman should have a gay and frivolous daughter.

Things cheered up a lot once Linda was home.

She turned the television on, though she didn't pay much attention to it. She mostly chattered to us while she ate. I sat nursing the kitten, taking comfort from his warmth and grace, and Debbie did the most talking. But when Linda had gone upstairs to get ready for her 'date' Debbie sank deep into her book, slumped in her favourite attitude, with her legs hanging sideways over one arm of the chair.

There was a lot of activity out in the kitchen and scullery by then, and Aunt Eileen's help, a woman called Mrs Tonkings, kept passing to and fro on the way to the students' dining-room. Presently I began to feel guilty and asked if I could help, and she seemed grateful.

The dining-room was at the front of the house and was a big, high room that had once been elegant. Now it was rather dismal, with mud-coloured curtains and a few dark paintings, but there was a glorious great cyclamen with about a dozen cerise flowers. It looked very exotic and quite unlike Aunt Eileen, and Mrs Tonkings told me that the American student had bought it.

Aunt Eileen came out of the kitchen looking hot and discovered Debbie reclining there like a lady, though she didn't seem to think her attitude very ladylike.

'Come on, girl. It may be different when you have homework to do, but I hate to see any one wasting their time when there's work to be done. Go and bang the gong, then you can help to carry things in.'

Debbie glared, pushing back her hair. Clearly she was coming back, with the greatest reluctance, from Margot Fonteyn's exciting, successful life.

'I'm sure your mum doesn't let you be idle, and her with two young children.'

'Unpaid labour. I told you,' Debbie muttered to me, as she slipped past. She banged the gong so fiercely that it could probably be heard in Bedford Square.

The students came thundering down the stairs, with a great deal of talk and laughter. I felt very shy when I went in with the potatoes, while Debbie followed with the hot plates. All talk stopped and they stared, then most of them smiled.

'Hullo!' said the red-haired girl, Sara. 'Got you working already, has she?'

'The students get younger every term,' said a pale young man, with a floppy piece of hair. He was Arthur Moorhead, we learned later.

'Ah, but these are ballet students. Going to the Lingeraux. Debbie and Dorrie Darke, isn't it?' Sara asked. 'Mrs Doom's nieces from the darkest North.'

'Shhh, you fool!'

'Is that what you call her?' Debbie asked, giggling. 'Mrs Doom? I must say it suits her.'

'Or Mrs Gloom,' said Sara, grinning. 'Only don't you go and split on us. She isn't a bad old thing, even though she does always look on the dark side.'

'That's what someone once said of Dorrie,' said

66

Debbie. ' "Darke by name and dark by nature."
And Aunt Eileen was born a Darke, I s'pose.'

'She has a secret face,' said Sara, staring at me, and
I came over shyer than ever and dropped some
potato on James MacDonald's trousers. He said it
didn't matter and they were certainly very old and
rather grubby trousers. He had a lovely voice, with
a kind of singing lilt.

It was quite *extraordinary* to be there. Ballet
students . . . us! With London wrapped in winter
darkness outside and the Lingeraux in the morning.
All the unfamiliar faces swam a little and I hoped
that I wasn't going to cry.

Home seemed so dreadfully far away and the
thought suddenly swamped me that we wouldn't see
Dad or Mother, or the young ones, for three months,
And we had nowhere of our own, nowhere to hide,
except for a rather depressing garret.

I wondered if Debbie felt the same. She was
smiling at Winston Marshall, the coloured student,
and, perhaps by contrast, she looked dazzlingly fair
and delicate, striking a slight attitude.

I couldn't stay there any longer. The faces really
were swimming in a mist of tears. I bolted up the
first broad flight of stairs and locked myself in the
first lavatory I came to, where I leaned against the
door and fought my grief and homesickness. Everything, I told myself, would be all right, really thrilling, in the morning.

My bed was dreadfully hard and I was cold. Aunt

Eileen, it seemed, didn't believe in hot water bottles, but I thought perhaps I would save up for one, or ask Mother to send an old one from home. About three in the morning the wind began to howl and I heard a soft brushing sound against the window. Debbie was sleeping peacefully; I could tell by her regular breathing. I wished that I could creep in with her, but for one thing there wasn't room in those narrow beds, and for another she wouldn't welcome me.

But I suppose I must have slept, for suddenly someone was thumping on the door. It was still dark, but my watch had a luminous dial (Dad had given us both cheap watches for our twelfth birthday) and it was half-past seven. Shivering, I groped for the light and the cheerless bulb immediately showed me the garret, with our Lingeraux uniforms laid out in readiness. Debbie groaned and burrowed deeper under the bedclothes.

'Light the fire, for heaven's sake!' she implored me.

I did so, then ran to the window. Snow was piled up on the sill outside and fresh flakes spattered the panes.

'It's been snowing nearly all night,' I said, dragging on my dressing-gown. The bathroom was on the floor below and was occupied. I stood leaning against some warm pipes, trying to stop shivering, until the door opened and Rachel came out, with her mousy hair on end and looking as though she hadn't washed much. All the dearer rooms had fitted basins, but none on the top floor boasted such a luxury.

We dressed in our new clothes and went down to breakfast through the wakening house. Arthur Moorhead had his radio on; he almost always did. It was like being in a dream, I thought, and not a very nice one, with so much lying immediately ahead. But the kitten was there on the rug, playing with a feather. How lovely to be a kitten, with no worries!

'Now make sure you've got everything,' Aunt Eileen said, when we came downstairs again just after eight-thirty, wearing our raincoats over our suits. Our coats would have been warmer, but it was snowing hard and they would only have got wet. Anyway, we had our lovely big fluffy blue scarves.

Debbie checked over her case: 'Towel, house slippers, ballet shoes, pencil box, mascot—'

'Mascot? You superstitious child!'

'All ballet dancers have mascots, Aunt Eileen. Mine is a little doll wearing a silver tutu. Dorrie has a wooden elephant someone gave her once.'

'I suppose you're going to put on your gum boots? There they are behind the door. You can keep them there always, but mind you wipe your feet well when you come in. Good-bye, then. Have a good day.'

We set off into the white, cold world. Gower Street was slushy and a bus almost immediately sent up a shower of dirty snow. We shrieked and tried to avoid the splashes. But Bedford Square was white in the centre and looked nice. The British Museum was touched with snow here and there and the bare trees in Bloomsbury Square were decorated with blobs of fluffy whiteness. The wind whipped the snow in our faces as we crossed towards the Lingeraux School.

There were a lot of boys and girls in blue raincoats or grey coats converging from all directions. Some of them looked quite old, sixteen or even older, and others were quite small. Debbie marched boldly towards the steps.

'Come on, Dorrie. Don't look so scared. Our school at home was far, far bigger than this.'

'It wasn't a ballet school, though. A London ballet school,' I said.

And then we were up the steps and in the shabby hall that I well remembered from that dreadful September day. Just to be there brought it all back to me, but I reminded myself that *that* trouble was all over and must be forgotten. Though it was going to be hard to forget entirely that I had had so many doubts about whether they wanted me for myself, or simply as a kind of appendage to Debbie.

The school was lovely and warm, anyway, and the cloakrooms smelt familiarly of wet gum boots, much used ballet shoes and cheap soap. We had been told to change into our practice clothes, as ballet classes for everyone would follow General Assembly, which apparently only took place once or twice a term at nine o'clock.

The boys' cloakrooms were at the other end of the

basement and they were making an awful noise. It seemed very strange to have boys in a school.

There seemed to be no familiar faces and I stuck close to Debbie as we went up again and followed everyone towards the hall. It seemed that we were to be in Class Four and we were told to sit about half-way up the hall. The young ones were in front and the older boys and girls behind. The senior students were in the two back rows and they looked nearly grown up and very grand and remote.

Debbie began chatting to her next door neigh-bour, but was shushed as the staff filed on to the platform. Madame Lingeraux was not there and Assembly was taken by the headmistress, Miss Sherwood. She greeted us, with a special word to the new pupils, then she read a lot of notices and finally we sang a hymn. I tried to pay attention, but I don't think I really did. I still couldn't believe that I was at the Lingeraux, really there; Dorrie Darke, with a scholarship.

I came alive in the ballet class. It was the only thing that I enjoyed in that whole long day. Our teacher was the Miss Verney who had shown us to the cloakrooms in September, and I knew at once that she was very good. She was little and dark and decisive, and you just had to pay attention all the time. I enjoyed the *barre* work and even the centre practice. It was like arriving at something familiar and dear after wandering in the wilderness.

Miss Verney asked our names at the beginning

and after that she made no remarks to us at all. She did say some very sharp things to a few of the girls (there were no boys in the class) and I knew that if she did it to me I should shrivel up. But then the class was over and we ran away to change without a word of criticism or praise being cast in our direction.

'Funny she ignored us,' said Debbie, and I wondered rather nastily if she had fully expected to be received as the shining wonder of the Lingeraux. But the Lingeraux, of course, wasn't the Grayland. In London we were amongst dozens of dedicated students, all of whom were probably grimly set on being ballerinas.

Our classroom was on the first floor, overlooking the square. There were twenty-five of us, twelve girls and thirteen boys, and still no familiar faces. I hadn't seen Mel at all and kept on hoping she would appear. She ought to be there as she had won a scholarship.

We were given time-tables and books by a Miss Lines. Then she went away and someone else came to take English literature—*As You Like It*. It is one of my favourite Shakespeare plays, so that was something else familiar, but I didn't feel relaxed. There were going to be so many things and people to remember, and, perhaps it was the bad night I had had, but I had a headache and heartache, too, because I still felt so far from home.

It seemed awful to have got my heart's desire and to be miserable.

Really the lessons were all right, and the teachers seemed kind and pleasant, but I was shy and out of things. It was particularly noticeable in break and worse during lunch, which we had in the canteen with all the others who stayed.

We seemed to be the only new girls in our class, but I hadn't even the comfort of Debbie, because she had already made friends with a little dark girl called Claudia Wood, who turned out to be Cécile Barreux's niece, and a foreign girl called Lotti Karl. There seemed to be a great many foreigners and I thought that that was going to be interesting. There was even a coloured girl in our class, Mary Ann Schulz. She seemed a great favourite and laughed a lot, and I hoped I should get to know her. I was puzzled about what would happen to her when she was older, because it didn't seem likely that she would fit easily into any ballet company.

Quite a lot of people spoke to me, but I felt tongue-tied and stupid and they soon went away. At lunch I sat next to a boy with a Russian name, Serge Something-or-other and he asked where I came from. I told him Birkenhead in Cheshire and pointed out Debbie, sitting at the other end of the table and laughing with Lotti Karl, and he asked: 'Is that your *sister*?' in the way I most disliked. And after that he talked to the boy on his other side.

It snowed all day. Sometimes I looked out at Bloomsbury Square and was stabbed with amazement that I was in London. I wished that Mel was

73

there, as she would have made all the difference, I thought, but there was still no sign of her.

At the end of afternoon school I gathered up my courage and stayed behind to speak to Miss Lines, who was piling up books to be marked. She smiled at me quite warmly.

'Did you want something, Doria?'

'Oh, please . . . at the audition there was a girl called Meldreth Forrest. She won a scholarship, too, but she isn't here.'

She hesitated, then took up her register.

'I think she must be the one—yes, here she is. She's got measles, I'm afraid. Hard luck, isn't it? Her mother sent a note, saying she won't be able to come for two weeks.'

'Oh, dear!' I felt dreadfully dismayed.

She put her hand on my shoulder for a moment.

'Well, cheer up. Two weeks will soon pass. You're one of the ones from the North, aren't you?'

'Yes, Birkenhead.'

'And homesick, I expect? You're not like your twin, are you? When I heard that there were twins I expected to have one of those silly experiences, not being able to tell one from another.'

'We're quite different,' I said.

When I went slowly down to the cloakrooms Debbie was nearly ready to leave. She said:

'Do hurry, Dorrie!'

But by the time I was ready she'd gone. When I reached the front steps she was crossing the square,

74

going away from Gower Street with Claudia, Lotti and two boys. So I walked home alone.

I looked at London in the snow and tried to tell myself how lucky I was. I was going to get to know it all ... some time soon I was going to the Royal Opera House and the Lingeraux Theatre. I was going to have all kinds of new experiences.

But I felt cold, lonely and hurt because Debbie had gone off without me, though really she usually had at home in Birkenhead, and it must be my own fault that I hadn't made friends.

Aunt Eileen had given me a key and I let myself in to the hall. There was no one about and I was thankful. I eased off my gum boots and put them side by side under the letter-rack, intending to move them later. I ran up the first flight of stairs in my stockinged feet, but on the landing above my spirits failed. Arthur Moorhead couldn't be in, because everywhere was very silent. I sat down on the first step of the next flight, in the shadows, and fought my desolation.

Then suddenly the door of the 'best' room opened and a flood of light came out, reaching me. Clyde Smith, the New Yorker, stood there, with some books under his arm.

'Hi Kid!' he said. 'What are you doing there?'

'Hi!' I answered hollowly and he came slowly towards me.

'What's the matter? You look kind of miserable. Homesick?'

75

He was so nice. He had a lovely quiet, drawly voice and crisp brown hair.

'Terribly,' I said. 'I—I—' and I burst into shameful tears.

He sat on the stair beside me. That flight was still pretty wide. And he held my hand.

'Where do you live? Is it far away?'

'T-Two hundred m-miles,' I told him, sniffing.

'Well, look! I guess it's pretty hard when you're so young, but how about me? *My* home is more than three thousand miles away.'

'But you're grown up,' I said, so surprised that I stopped crying.

He laughed.

'Don't tell me that you believe all feeling stops just because one reaches the ripe old age of twenty-one?'

I had believed it. I thought it must be lovely to be grown up and beyond suffering.

'It can't be so bad.'

'We-ell, it's just possible to feel something, you know. When one is some place far from home. I like London, but I've only been here one week. I guess I don't know many people yet.'

I thought of New York; it always looked so fabulous in pictures. High and gleaming, in clear light.

'I—I shan't see them all at home for three months.'

'And I'm not going home for a year, maybe

longer. Two exiles, you see. How would it be if we took a walk and explored one Saturday?'

'It would be lovely,' I said, suddenly feeling better. 'I can read a map. I've got one.'

I went up to the garret still feeling snuffly and rather damp, but not so sunk in self-pity.

* 7 *

New Friends and Covent Garden

Debbie was late for tea. She came in looking glowing, with snow all over her scarf and making her hair look even more silvery than usual.

'We thought you were lost,' Aunt Eileen said, a little tartly, and Debbie flung down her case, shook her beret and answered cheerfully:

'Oh, no. I walked some of the way home with Claudia. She lives in a flat over in Bayswater. Then I tried to get the bus back, but it was the rush hour, so I had to walk.'

'Well, I'd sooner you came straight home while it gets dark so early. After all, you're a stranger to London, and if anything happened to you ... besides, I suppose you have homework to do?'

'Yes, a horrid lot. I think it's mean on the first day.'

'Well, get your tea and then clear one end of the table. It won't be an ideal arrangement, with people in and out, but I can't have you using light and heat somewhere else.'

Debbie ate heartily, casting occasional glances at

me, but not asking any direct questions. She chattered to Aunt Eileen, telling her some of the happenings of the day. But when we had cleared the table as ordered, and were settling ourselves with our books, she asked:

'Where'd you get to? I waited for you on the steps.'

'You were going off with the others when I saw you,' I said, and she must have caught something in my tone because she answered rather defensively:

'I thought you were being slow on purpose. You didn't seem to want to be friendly with anyone. Why are you always so miserable?'

'I'm not. I didn't mean to be. I stayed to ask Miss Lines something. I can't help being shy.'

'Shy! You looked just awfully dumb,' she said unkindly, and I buried my face in my Shakespeare preparatory to writing an essay on my favourite character in *As You Like It*. For two pins I could have cried again, but I was determined not to. For one thing I had to get on with my work, because I didn't mean to disgrace myself at the Lingeraux that way, even if I wasn't going to turn out a popular person. Only sometimes I looked at Debbie's bent fair head and wondered how on earth we were ever going to get close to each other again. It *must* partly be my fault, I thought.

When we were getting ready for bed I said to her:

'But Debbie, didn't you feel out of things a bit, sometimes? Most of them *do* seem much better off than we are, and there was such a lot of talk that was different from the Grammar School. They seem so— so much more sophisticated in some ways, and we don't really know anything about the Company and all the things that—'

'We'll soon learn,' said Debbie, diving into bed. 'Of course we'll learn. Oh, I *loved* it, all that glorious gossip, and foreigners and boys. And Claudia was so friendly, even though she's been at the Lingeraux for two years and has a lot of friends. I expect I shall meet Cécile Barreux and—'

'Was that why? I mean why you got to know *her?*'

Debbie looked at me brightly over the sheet.

'Well, no, not really. I liked her at once and she liked me. It was sheer luck. But I'd sooner know the important ones, because I mean to be an important one myself. I don't mean to be in the background.'

'You won't,' I said.

'Very catty all of a sudden, Dorrie Darke. I don't like that tone.' But she was half-laughing.

'Not really meant to be catty,' I mumbled. 'But— aren't you homesick at *all?*'

She was silent for some moments, then she said:

'I wasn't in school all day. I felt as though it was the place where I just had to be. As though it were fore-ordained. But when I'd left Claudia I felt a bit queer. It was in Oxford Street, and the snow came on again and there were such crowds, everyone pushing along with umbrellas up. And I couldn't get on a bus. To tell you the truth I wasn't even sure what bus it should be. And I felt as though I might be invisible; just a dot amongst eight million people, or however many there are in London. A man nearly knocked me down and he glared as though it was my fault. I—I did feel homesick then.'

Well, that was something. I could very easily imagine her in Oxford Street, alone and bewildered.

I snuggled down in bed, clutching the blessed comfort of a very old, rather smelly hot water bottle. For Aunt Eileen had relented and found them for us, saying that it was colder than usual and she supposed it was all right to coddle ourselves, but not to blame her if we got chilblains. As neither of us had ever had a chilblain in our lives it was a risk we were more than willing to take.

The next morning the Lingeraux did seem more familiar. We had our own pegs in the cloakroom, and we knew which studio and classroom to go to. And the ballet class was just as enjoyable as on the previous day. While I was doing those familiar exercises I felt at peace with the world and with myself.

Miss Verney still took no particular notice of us, but when I was leaving the studio—one of the last to go—she suddenly said to me, smiling:

'You've been well taught, dear. There's very little to unlearn.'

To *me* she said it, not to Debbie, and I went to the cloakroom on wings, for a time, at least, believing that they had wanted me for myself. Some of the pleasure and relief lasted until break, when I felt shy and lonely again. It was interesting to listen to the gossip, certainly, but I felt rather like Debbie in Oxford Street, almost invisible. They seemed to know a great deal about every member of the Company and names flew about. The names of senior students, too, for a lot of the girls in our class seemed to be keen on the older boys. Lotti blushed every time a certain Joseph Bartol was mentioned.

If I'd just pushed myself into a group and talked, the way Debbie did, I knew I'd probably be accepted at once, but somehow I couldn't. I had been smitten with an awful kind of tongue-tiedness.

After lunch I could stand being alone in the crowd no longer, so I slipped away from the merry groups in the canteen and the lower corridors. In fine weather, I had heard, most people strolled in Bloomsbury Square, but it was too cold to go out.

So I climbed stairs and more stairs, peeping into classrooms and an occasional studio, though most of the studios were out at the back. Once I came upon a group of little ones, all giggling and silly, and once I looked into a classroom I had thought was empty and found myself facing three big girls, sitting in earnest conversation on the hot pipes. I knew they must be senior students because their blue-lined cloaks lay over a chair. Only the senior students had them.

I fled on, climbing some more stairs that reminded me of the ones that led to our garret, and then I was up in what seemed to be storerooms. The second one

I looked into was full of music, tidily stacked on shelves, and case after case of records, all, as far as I could see, of ballet music. There were also several record players up there and I was just wondering if I dare put on a record and play it softly when someone sneezed.

The sound came from behind one of the music shelves and when I looked round the corner I was startled to discover a boy of about my own age. He looked rather red and self-conscious and I realised quite quickly that I had seen him in the classroom, but not noted him particularly.

'Hullo!' he said awkwardly, and seeing someone so obviously on the defensive helped me a great deal.

'Hullo,' I answered. 'Were you hiding?'

'We-ell, I was exploring, and then I heard you coming and didn't know who it was. Not many places where one can be alone, are there?'

When I heard his voice I knew that he was not a Londoner, but certainly from the North and quite possibly from Manchester. We had a girl from Manchester in our class at the Grammar School.

'Are you new?' I asked. It hadn't occurred to me until then to wonder about new boys.

'I am that.'

'From Manchester?'

His rather nice grey eyes flew open.

'Now that's clever, lass. How did you know?'

I laughed.

'I'm a witch. I come from Birkenhead.'

We eyed each other with growing understanding, and he said slowly:

'You're new, too. I saw you in class. You read a bit of your essay out loud this morning. It was jolly good. And at lunch you weren't talking.'

'I'm homesick and I don't know what to say to them yet. Not like Debbie, my sister. She's just— just thrown herself into it.'

'Is she in the same class?'

'Yes. She sits next to me, at the moment. Not for long, I expect. She's my twin, but we don't look alike.'

'I didn't notice her,' he said, which gave him a high mark, if only he'd known it. He was going on: 'It's pretty grim at first, isn't it? Miles from home. Do you know London well?'

'I hardly know it at all, but I mean to,' I told him. 'We've been to London two or three times. Last time was just for two nights, for the audition. The time before was quite a long time ago, one summer. It was terribly hot and Mother was tired, so we didn't see very much, just went on the river or sat in the parks. Debbie and I were upset because there wasn't any ballet on *at all*. But I do mean to make up for it.'

'I was that thrilled when I won a scholarship, even though my dad was against it. Dad says it's no life for a boy, but I've always been keen on dancing. And I tell him they gave dancers double rations in Russia during the war. They *respect* 'em in Russia. Dad says Britain's good enough for him, but he wouldn't stop me coming. The old man's not bad. Only now I'm here—'

'We'll learn to find our way about,' I said, and then I told him about Aunt Eileen's, including the students and our chilly garret. He in turn told me that he was living with his mother's first cousin up near St Pancras Station. The cousin was married and they kept a greengrocery business.

'Got to earn my keep by doing some delivering on Saturday mornings,' he was just saying when we both jumped about a foot in the air because the bell for lessons sounded far below. At the same moment there were footsteps outside our little storeroom and, horror of horrors, who should appear in the doorway but Madame Lingeraux herself.

She stood there staring at us in a very formidable way. She looked about as broad as she was long in a big fur coat and snow-boots and it was really extremely hard to imagine her as ever being quite a great dancer, though later, when I saw her moving in her quick way, I realized that she had, strangely, kept some of the grace of a dancer.

I'm sure I went pale, and the boy, whose name I still didn't know, certainly did. The bright, rather stern glance swept over us.

'Now who are you? No, don't tell me. I never forget a face. Peter Lumb. That's right, isn't it? The scholarship boy from Manchester. And Doria Darke.'

'Yes, Madame,' I said shakily, remembering the

85

way she had clasped my hand at that terrible interview. *She* had given me my scholarship . . . she had made it possible for me to come to London. And now I was disgraced, caught where I probably had no right to be, and late for the next lesson to boot. All my bitter uncertainty was back, because somehow my behaviour was all the worse if she had given me that scholarship because of Debbie.

But then I realised with amazement that she was smiling, not looking cross at all.'

'So you came? You and that fair sister of yours? Hum! And what are you doing up here? Looking for somewhere where you could be homesick in peace?'

Well, I'd said I was a witch, but *she* certainly was. It was a relief, anyway, that she understood and hadn't thought we were up to mischief.

'Yes, Madame. I—I—everything feels so strange, and—and I came up here and Peter was here first.'

'So you've made friends? Well, that's a start, isn't it? I suppose your sister's made plenty of friends already?'

A witch indeed, I was surprised by her accurate character reading after only meeting us once, months ago.

'She isn't shy.'

'I could see that. An extrovert type, if ever there was one. It makes life easier. Well, now you're late for afternoon school, so you'd better explain that you were talking to me. No, wait a minute. Find me the case of *Swan Lake* records, will you? You're better

86

able to bend than I am, especially with this coat on.'

We scrabbled round helpfully for a few moments and it was Peter who found it. Then we more or less backed out, not exactly bowing, but feeling that we ought to. My face was burning by then.

'She was *nice*!' I gasped, as we hurried down the stairs.

'I thought she'd blow us sky high,' said Peter. Then, as we reached our classroom door: 'I'll walk home with you after school, if you like.'

'Oh, thank you,' I said, and we made our late entry, which was rather embarrassing as everyone looked up to stare. They stared harder than ever when we explained that we had been talking to Madame Lingeraux. Debbie looked as though she thought I'd be in trouble.

I sank down and took out my new arithmetic book, but it was a little time before I could concentrate. Debbie, an extrovert type. What on earth did it mean? I resolved to look it up in the dictionary just as soon as I had the chance.

During afternoon break, which was only five minutes, Peter came over to talk to me, and after school he was waiting in the hall, wearing his grey Lingeraux overcoat and blue scarf. He was quite a tall boy and reasonably good-looking, with curly brown hair.

Debbie was just behind with Claudia, Lottie and some others, and I waved to her casually as I went off. It was wonderful to have a friend and not to have to tag on to Debbie's companions. London looked quite different as we idled our way along Great Russell Street.

'Ever been into the British Museum?' asked Peter, as we passed that vast building, its lights shining through the snowy gloom.

'Never,' I told him.

'Never mind, lass. We'll go one day,' he said, and we grinned at each other.

It was nice to think that I had two friends with whom I might explore London.

It was certainly much better at the Lingeraux now that I had a friend. Peter and I sat together in the canteen and talked quite hard, and, hearing us, those on either side and opposite began to join in. So I was no longer dumb Dorrie Darke, though I was still often quiet and sometimes, all through that week, I was visited by dreadful homesickness and terrible doubts. I suppose I just had no confidence in myself at all.

But all the strange faces were beginning to grow clearer. I could now recognise the much admired Joseph Bartol when he walked along the hall and I knew the names of other senior students. I knew all the names in my class, too, and had learned to recognise most of the members of staff.

On Friday afternoon after school Peter and I went to look at the other studios and the Company rehearsal rooms a couple of streets away, and, as luck would have it, some of the members of the Company were just coming out. We stood in the snowy street watching them walk away or pile into cars. Cécile Barreux was there, muffled up in scarves and a huge sheepskin jacket, not very glamorous, really, but it was wonderful to see her off the stage, a real live human being. She was with the principal dancer, Michael Mann.

'Some day that might be us,' I said, but it seemed an impossibility.

We walked all the way down Kingsway in the teeth of a bitter wind. The lights were shining out, the red buses sped past, and it was London ... London. We turned into a side street and stood in front of the little Lingeraux Theatre, looking at the posters and the photographs of the dancers. But then I remembered that Aunt Eileen might be cross at my staying out, when it was so cold and already dark, and we walked back at top speed. Some of the new high buildings were a blaze of light by then and I wondered if Clyde thought that London sometimes looked a little like New York. But some of those Manhattan buildings rose seventy or even a hundred storeys; I could scarcely imagine seeing structures so high in the sky.

When I let myself into the house in Gower Street and began to climb up to the garret to leave my things I heard my name called. Clyde had evidently been on the look out for me, because his door was open and he jumped up from his desk and came out on to the landing.

89

'Hi, Dorrie! How'd you like to go to the Royal Opera House tomorrow afternoon?'

I gaped at him.

'Covent Garden? Oh, I'd love to. It's one of the dreams of my life to go there. But—But you'd never get tickets!'

He laughed, showing his good teeth.

'You underestimate Americans! I have them already. Matinées are easier than evening performances and I thought your aunt might kind of object to your being out late. It's *Coppélia*. How's that?'

'It's *wonderful*!' I gasped. 'But perhaps Aunt Eileen—'

'Now don't you worry about your aunt.' He pronounced it 'ant' as we did, though I had noticed that everyone in the South said it differently. 'She says you may go. Let me tell you something, Dorrie. She's not half as bad as she seems.'

'But Debbie—Debbie's dying to go to Covent Garden, too.'

'I asked her and she said she wasn't free. I guess she can go some other time. Is it a date for tomorrow?'

'Oh, yes!' I agreed fervently. It was only four days since I had sat on the stairs and cried and now I had two friends and was going to Covent Garden. It was a kind of cumulative thing, like those old fairy stories. Next week I might have three friends and go to the Lingeraux Theatre. It went a long way to making up for homesickness and cold and not being able to stick up our art reproductions. For Aunt Eileen had said it would spoil the wallpaper.

I stumped up the rest of the stairs, humming the mechanical toys music from *Coppélia* under my breath.

* 8 *

The Arrival of Mel

Debbie was furious about Covent Garden. She stormed and almost cried, until Aunt Eileen, who witnessed the scene, spoke to her very sharply.

'It isn't poor Dorrie's fault. How can you carry on like that, a great girl of thirteen?'

Debbie calmed down a little.

'I *know* it isn't Dorrie's fault. It's all Clyde Smith's. Of course he *did* ask if I was free, but I thought he was just asking me to go exploring with him and Dorrie. Dorrie told me they were going to, one day. And Claudia *had* asked me to tea. But I could have gone another Saturday. I've been living to go to the Opera House.'

'Well,' I said slowly, and it cost me a lot, 'you'd better go instead of me. I don't suppose that Clyde will mind, and—'

But, at that, Aunt Eileen interfered, and I must admit that I was glad she did. I'm not really all that much of a martyr, and I'd been living for it, too.

'No, Dorrie, you are to go and enjoy yourself. It's only polite, anyway, when Clyde got the ticket for you. And Debbie has already accepted Claudia's invitation.'

So that was that, but it made me rather miserable and quite spoilt my keen anticipation. I didn't want any more trouble between Debbie and me.

She sulked for the rest of the evening, scarcely speaking when we went to bed, and the next morning she wasn't a bit keen on helping Aunt Eileen. I wasn't all that keen, either, but there was no escaping it and I suppose it was only fair. But it was rather hard luck when it was such a frosty, brilliant morning, with London waiting to be explored.

First of all she made us clean our own room, saying that the daily woman had enough to do, then she set Debbie to polishing some silver and brass and asked me to tidy and dust the sitting-room. Linda came down at ten o'clock, wearing a scarlet sweater, a black skirt so tight that she could hardly move, and huge ear-rings. She grinned at us and said:

'Gosh! Industrious kids! I suppose there's some coffee left?'

Aunt Eileen glared at her daughter.

'Not a drop. Everything's cleared away. I thought you were stopping there till lunchtime.'

'No, I'm going shopping,' Linda said amiably. 'Well, I suppose you'll be having elevenses soon, or I can go and get something in the nearest coffee bar.'

'Do that,' said Aunt Eileen. 'You're only in the way when there's work to be done.' And Linda laughed, patted her on the shoulder, and ran back upstairs. But she was so gay and casual that somehow one didn't resent the fact that she never helped. I didn't, anyhow, and I suspected that Aunt Eileen didn't mind all that much. It was growing increasingly evident that, in spite of the tone she sometimes took, she was secretly proud of Linda.

Aunt Eileen presently said that she was going to do some household shopping and we could go with her, if we liked, to learn just where to go, when it was our turn. Debbie said she would sooner stop at home, but I was glad to get out. There were no shops very near, but Aunt Eileen said it was cheaper, in any case, to get a bus and go to Soho.

'Of course, a lot of the things are delivered, but I like to look for bargains.'

Oxford Street was crowded with Saturday morning shoppers and pretty horrid, but very soon we were in Berwick Street and that was much nicer. I loved the whole atmosphere and was fascinated by the market stalls, but Aunt Eileen marched me firmly into a small self-service store, then into various other small shops. Clearly she was well known and was treated respectfully. She was the kind of person no one would dare to rob of as much as a halfpenny. In some of the shops she introduced me as her niece and explained that she would sometimes be sending me to buy things. One woman called me 'Ducks' and gave me a chocolate biscuit.

There were a lot of foreigners about, and a good many shops selling foreign food, but we avoided those, for Aunt Eileen said she had no time for 'fancy foreign stuff'. It was all the greatest fun and Aunt Eileen surprised me by buying me an ice cream.

'Seems absurd to me, with snow and frost on the ground, but young people have strong stomachs. Let's hope it doesn't spoil your lunch, though.

I had to have rather a hurried lunch, anyhow, because the ballet started at two. Clyde had very long legs and walked extremely fast, so it didn't take long to reach the Opera House. And, as soon as we drew near, all my vague guilt over Debbie faded away. It was so wonderful and exciting to be approaching Floral Street, breathing the smell of earth and carrots on the icy air. Later I realised that there always a country smell about Covent Garden Market and it was always bound up with ballet in my mind.

Crowds of people were hurrying along the narrow street, in the shadow of the Opera House, and suddenly I realised that we were passing the stage door. The stage door of the Royal Opera House! Often, perhaps, I could come there after a performance and see the great ones.

Then we came to the gallery entrance and I halted, but was surprised to find Clyde's hand on my elbow, steering me onwards round to the front.

'Not this time,' he said, laughing. 'I guess I thought that as it's the first time for both of us we'd do things in style.'

It was just wonderful to be with a handsome, *rich*

American, and I tried to walk with dignity as we entered the building, so warm and luxurious after the cold air outside. We went down a passage and then up some stairs, and suddenly we were in the vast, semi-circular auditorium, with its tiers rising to the high, domed roof and the great red and gold curtain.

Clyde bought two programmes and asked if I would like some candy.

'Oh, no, thank you,' I said, trying not to sound shocked, for of course he meant to be kind. But Debbie and I had long ago decided that it was terrible to eat in a theatre. We always minded when people made loud rustling sounds just at the most important moment of a ballet. But he seemed to understand, for he grinned.

'You could have eaten it during the intermission.'

Our seats were in the stalls circle, in the front row, and it seemed astonishing luxury. I stared all around, scarcely able to believe that I was really *there* at last. Then I settled down to study the programme, finding out who was dancing each rôle. It was not the first time I had seen *Coppélia*; I had once seen it in Liverpool, but it hadn't been a very good production.

Now it was marvellous. I was lost in enchantment even before the curtain rose. I sat there in the warm darkness, as the conductor took his place and the overture began. And then there was the huge brilliantly lighted stage and the village scene. Dr Coppelius's house was on the right and there was the mechanical doll, Coppélia, on the balcony, so realistic that everyone thought her a beautiful girl. A very famous ballerina was dancing Swanilda and I watched every perfect movement intently, for I had never been lucky enough to see her before.

The lively peasant dances . . . Swanilda's quarrel with Franz, because he was attracted to the un-known girl on the balcony . . . the dropping of the key to Dr Coppelius's work-shop . . . I watched it all without missing a single movement. I had forgotten Clyde beside me, everything but the ballet. Though once I smelt a cold, woody fragrance from the stage, that stage that was bigger than any I had ever seen, and I thought fleetingly: 'It's *Covent Garden*!'

In the first interval we went up into the Crush Bar, so beautiful with its chandelier and flowers and mirrors, and I found that Clyde didn't really know much about ballet. I could tell him quite a lot and he listened most respectfully and really seemed interested.

'But you must have seen some ballet in New York,' I said.

'We-ell, a little, I guess. Sometimes I go to dance companies at the State Theatre or City Centre, but I never knew the names for the movements. It's real nice to have a genuine ballet student to explain.'

That was the best thing about Clyde. He never treated me as though I were just a child.

'I'll give you a demonstration one day,' I promised. 'Then you really will know an arabesque and a fouetté.'

97

It was during the third act, while Prayer was dancing her solo, that everything suddenly fused into a
huge, overpowering feeling of awareness and happiness. The misery of the past week seemed unimportant then, for it had all led to this. Watching that
lovely dancing, I knew more certainly than ever
before that somehow I had to be a dancer, a *good*
dancer. It even seemed possible that I might turn
into a ballerina, if I worked hard. Though one side
of me knew, even in those exalted moments, that
work alone wouldn't do it. Debbie might have that
rare, precious spark, and I might not. I almost
prayed that it might be in me, too, somewhere,
deeply hidden.

I couldn't say much at first as we came out into the
cold, dark streets. I was still remembering the clapping and the flowers, the whole atmosphere of the
Opera House, and, above all, the dancing. I came to
myself when I realised that we had passed Covent
Garden Tube Station and were heading away along
Long Acre.

'This isn't the way home.'

'No, I know. I'm taking you to have tea. Your
aunt said it would be O.K.,' Clyde told me.

We went to the New Arts Theatre Club. Clyde
signed the book and we climbed the stairs.

'I'm a member,' he explained. 'I joined last week.'

We had tea sitting by a window from which I
could look down into Great Newport Street and over
to the busy point where six streets meet. The lights

glittered and everywhere looked very busy and gay.

I poured out and tried to behave in an assured, grown up way. I heard a woman say: 'That's the Lingeraux uniform. The ballet school, you know. Smart, isn't it?' And I knew she meant me.

After that afternoon, though I was still often homesick and rather unhappy, I never really wished we had stayed safely at home in Birkenhead. I had seen a wider and more satisfying world.

During the next week the Lingeraux continued to present problems and I did find life a strain. I had not quite settled down to the methods of work—school work, I mean—and there were times when I still felt shy and out of things. But having Peter for a friend did help.

Debbie seemed to feel no strain at all and it was quite clear to me that she certainly wasn't going to have to take a back seat. She was always with the most important boys and girls in the class, she laughed a lot and seemed to take part effortlessly in their conversations. When she didn't know something, or had to confess that she had never been abroad, she said casually: 'Poor me, I'm from the darkest North and we haven't much money.' And she smiled in her winning way, tossing her pale, shining hair.

I wished I could behave just the way she did, for it obviously worked. It wasn't that I wanted to hide the fact that we were quite poor, but I *was* sometimes burningly conscious that we had missed things, that we came from a dreadfully narrow world. It was obvious, even in the things that were discussed casually and sensibly. Dad and Mother would have been shocked. Yet I could see already that that was a wrong attitude.

Peter felt much the same, I knew. Our backgrounds were similar. The point was that Debbie was totally unself-conscious and she was much quicker than me at adapting herself to the new atmosphere.

Yet, curiously, I was much happier at Aunt Eileen's than she was. I was finding that I *liked* the house in Gower Street, even the garret, though it continued to be cold and rather cheerless. I found the students absolutely fascinating and was surprised that they were so nice to me.

Sara asked me to her room, which was hung with pictures of famous actors and actresses, and the book shelves held many plays. We made coffee on her gas-ring and she told me about R.A.D.A. and her hopes for the future. Of course her fears were something like mine; of not being good enough, of not being able to make a living at the end of her training. She acted bits of plays for me and I sat on a cushion, entranced by Lady Macbeth, Ophelia and Puck. When I was leaving she said I could borrow all the plays I wanted, as long as I was sure to return them.

Rachel was nice to me, too. We got friendly during the second week in rather an odd way. Because I found *her* crying on the stairs—a future scientist and almost grown up, fancy!—and I sat beside her, not quite knowing what to say or do. But I soon found, when we had moved to the privacy of her room, that all I needed to do was listen. Her boy friend had deserted her for a girl who worked in a big store.

'And she hasn't any *brains*, Dorrie. I know that; I met her once. But she's terribly smart and pretty. Anyhow, I suppose men don't like women with brains. Oh, I wish I were dead!' But she did cheer up a little when we had made some coffee on *her* gas-ring and she told me about her home in Birmingham and her brothers and sisters and her dog called Dash.

Gradually I learned bits about the other students. Maribel Brown, who was studying commercial subjects, was mad keen on photography and had taken some lovely London pictures. Winston Marshall told me about his home in Jamaica, and perhaps best of all I liked to hear about the remote Hebridean island, Barra, where James MacDonald lived. It sounded so alien and beautiful and wild and I quite forgot London while he talked in his soft, sing-song voice. I had met him in Bloomsbury Street and we walked along together.

The nicest thing about *all* of them was that they didn't treat me as a child, but as a fellow student who had her way to make. Just being with them, and listening to them, taught me an enormous lot.

Linda was always fun. She often said very droll things and the constant procession of boy friends made each evening interesting. We never knew which one would turn up to take her out and I always hoped that two wouldn't arrive at the same time and perhaps fight it out in our presence. Linda was certainly frivolous, and of course hadn't the brains of the students, but she had what Aunt Eileen once called 'native wit' and was really no fool. She was just determined to enjoy herself.

'All this talk about atom bombs and world troubles makes me sick,' she said once. 'I'm alive now, aren't I? And young and pretty. It's really all that matters. Of course I *hate* to think of starving children, or what might happen after an atomic war, so I *don't* think about them. I can't do anything, anyway. Can you see *me* sitting down in Trafalgar Square, or taking part in one of those protest marches?'

'No, I can't, Miss,' said Aunt Eileen, overhearing the end of this speech. 'Not in those shoes, *or* in your lack of sensible underclothes. You'd get your death if you sat down for five minutes.'

'I mean to stay alive,' retorted her daughter and executed quite a good arabesque. She was wearing jeans that time, not a tight skirt. 'I could even be a ballet dancer if I tried.'

'You stick to earning your living in a sensible way,' said her mother. 'There are enough actresses and dancers in this house.'

I liked Aunt Eileen more and more. She certainly deserved her nicknames of 'Mrs Gloom' and 'Mrs Doom', for if there was a dark side she would certainly look on it, but even that was rather amusing and endearing, especially in contrast to Linda. The students played a game of what they called 'Doomisms', in which they tried to see who could make the most miserable and hopeless remark, but they didn't really mean to be unkind. They were all fond of her.

She was really very good to them, and when Arthur Moorhead was ill after having some teeth out she looked after him like a mother.

The only thing that Aunt Eileen and I had trouble about was Ruari. I just loved that kitten and we hadn't been in the house a week before he was finding his way up to our garret and sleeping on my bed. Sometimes *in* my bed, as the nights were still bitterly cold. Aunt Eileen found out and threatened dire things to me and Ruari if it happened again. But you can't keep a clever, comfort-loving kitten away from a nice warm bed in winter, and in the end she turned a blind eye, after saying:

'Well, if you want to catch some unpleasant disease you're going the right way about it, girl. I heard of someone once who developed terrible skin trouble after letting her cat sleep on her bed.'

A typical 'Doomism', but as though I could catch anything, when Ruari was such a delicious, clean kitten, who washed himself all over about twenty times a day. He was growing and looked perfectly enchanting, with quite a thick bush of a tail that he always carried high, proudly.

Debbie got on with the students all right—they

obviously liked her—but she and Aunt Eileen just didn't hit it off. Debbie was always fighting her and trying to get out of things, with the result that Aunt Eileen probably gave her more tasks than she would have done otherwise and there was a constant atmosphere of sulks and argument.

'I wish you didn't suck up to her so,' she said crossly, one night.

'I don't,' I said, distressed. 'I don't mean to, Debbie. I like her, and she's really awfully good to us.'

Debbie grunted and burrowed down in bed. Bedtimes were never chatty affairs; never had been since we came to London, or really long before that.

Sometimes I lay awake feeling dreadfully miserable because Debbie and I were still so far from each other. I missed the old days still, when we had been friends and could say things to each other. But I couldn't think of anything that would help matters, and in my heart I hadn't really forgiven Debbie for all the awful things she had said in September.

Debbie was near the top of the class at the end of the second week at the Lingeraux and her eyes sparkled with triumph.

'Soon I'll be first, you'll see, Dorrie.'

I was tenth, which I suppose wasn't bad, but all the same I felt depressed. I had one of my familiar moods, when I decided that it wasn't worth trying to compete with Debbie. I'd always played second fiddle, anyway.

On Saturday afternoon the whole of our class went to the Lingeraux Theatre to see *Checkmate*, *L'Après-Midi d'un Faune*, and the revival of a ballet choreographed by Madame Lingeraux. Peter and I sat together and we both liked *Checkmate* best. Cécile Barreux was the Black Queen and the Bliss music was very exciting. The Lingeraux was a beautiful little red and gold theatre, very tiny after the Opera House, and I wondered if I should ever dance on that stage.

Suddenly, right in the middle of *L'Après-Midi*, I went cold with horror, as I thought of Debbie being accepted as a member of the Company and me not. It would be ten times worse than that business of the audition. It would be unbearable, for what *else* could I do with my life if I couldn't dance? The old, old problem of the young ballet student, as I knew even then, but it didn't help to think of all the people before me who had had to face and conquer rejection.

Something of that horror remained with me all through Sunday, which was too windy and snowy to go out, and when I got up on the Monday morning I wasn't greatly looking forward to the coming week, But I had forgotten about Mel.

She came into the cloakroom when I had just tied my ballet shoes. She was flushed from the cold, her hair was in a short, tidy pony-tail and she looked shy and hesitant. When she saw me her face broke into a wide smile.

'Oh, thank heaven! Dorrie, isn't it? I hoped and hoped you'd be here to hold my hand. Wasn't it awful getting measles so near the beginning of term? I cried like anything because fate had been so unkind.'

'I missed you,' I told her, realising, with a rush of wild relief, that she was just as nice as I remembered. 'I asked about you on the first day.'

'And what's it like? Have you made hordes of friends? Can you keep up with the dancing and the school work? Is it very terrifying?' She was changing rapidly as she fired off these questions.

I told her what I could as we went up the stairs, and on our way to the studio we met Peter, so I introduced them, hoping that they would like each other. I had already told Peter all I remembered about Mel.

Mel's presence made the most astonishing difference. Debbie had moved to sit with Lotti, so Mel was able to sit next to me and I was told to help her to try and catch up with the work. She was shy at first, though not, of course, with me or Peter, and before three days had passed I knew that she was going to make the most satisfactory of friends. She was so warm-hearted and understanding; funny, too. She was also a Londoner and could tell Peter and me a great deal. She promised to go around with us at week-ends or in the evenings, just as soon as it was light enough.

For a start she asked both of us to go to tea with

her on Saturday, but before that, on the Friday after
school, I went with her to the top of one of those
high, new buildings. It happened unexpectedly
because I had said how much they fascinated me and
she explained that she had an aunt who was an
office cleaner and who had just got a new job cleaning
the top floor of the Dunthorp Building, near Hay-
market.

Peter couldn't go, because he had to hurry home
to help in the shop, so Mel and I had tea, a sandwich
and a bun in a coffee bar (Aunt Eileen had grumbled
that she didn't know why I wanted to stay out in that
bitter weather, but she supposed it was an opportunity, so long as the lift didn't stick or something
worse) and then we walked through the rush-hour
crowds.

It was frosty and stars glittered above the lighted
streets. The endless traffic whirled around Piccadilly
Circus, and I suppose I must have begun to identify
myself with Londoners, because I didn't feel in the
least alien in those hurrying crowds. I felt as though
I belonged, had a right to be there.

The Dunthorp Building, every huge window a
blaze of light, towered high above the lesser buildings.

'Twenty-four storeys,' said Mel, craning her neck
and then promptly banging into a man with a brief-
case and a rolled umbrella. She recoiled, with apolo-
gies, and, giggling slightly, I said:

'Clyde Smith laughs at our skyscrapers.'

'Still, we'll get a lovely view, and we can't all be New Yorkers.'

She led the way through the swing doors and we stared up the huge, modern entrance hall—the lobby, Clyde would have called it. It was after half-past five and most of the office workers had gone. Cleaners were already hurrying on their way and Mel's aunt arrived a few minutes after us; a small, dumpy woman, with a good-humoured face and a cheerful Cockney voice.

'There you are, ducks! This your friend? Well, let's get on up. Only, mind you, you'll have to behave or I'll get shot. No poking into things as don't concern you.'

'We always behave,' said Mel demurely. 'We just want to see the view. Dorrie does, particularly. She comes from the North.'

Mrs Forrest clicked her tongue.

'I don't hold with building up to the sky, but there's no doubt these modern places make less work. In there, ducks. Press 24.'

The lift rose smoothly, silently, up and up. It was very exciting, I thought. And then we emerged into a long, gleaming corridor, with offices on either side. Mrs Forrest went off to find her brushes and cleaning materials, but before she went she said:

'I start in No. 1 and work my way along. You can go and look from that window at the end. It's a door really and opens on to a terrace. If you go out there be sure and close it after you. Only don't stay out there long, or you'll freeze your noses off and maybe get me into a row as well.'

We walked away along the corridor towards the glass door. Beyond it lights glittered, the lights of London.

* 9 *

Debbie Determined to be Noticed

We pushed open the door and went out on to the high terrace of the Dunthorp Building, and, the moment we saw the view, I quite forgot the intense cold.

'Oh, Mel! Mel!' I cried.

We were looking east and south and it was wonderful, beautiful. It was all outspread; Trafalgar Square ... the Mall ... Whitehall ... all picked out with lights. We could see the Embankment and the river, with the Shell Building rising, flood-lit, beyond. Then Waterloo Bridge, and far away, St Paul's.

It was a dream city on that frosty winter night and I loved it with all my heart.

'Not bad,' said Mel, with the calm of one who has always known it. 'But then we haven't seen New York or even Paris.'

'We might—if we ever become real dancers,' and then, perhaps because we were all alone, and staring at that view of London, I went on: 'Oh, I could be so happy if only—if only—'

'If only what?' asked Mel, not looking at me. 'I knew there was something. You may as well tell me.'

'And you won't tell a living soul? Not Peter, not anyone?'

''Course I won't. Cross my heart.'

So then I told her the whole story, standing there high on the Dunthorp Building. There was no wind and we were warmly wrapped up; I was glad she didn't suggest going in. Light spilled through the glass door and from a window near by, but we seemed very much alone.

I told her all about Debbie and me and how I had felt for a long time that Debbie was the better looking and far the better dancer, the one who was going to go far. And about what happened at the audition after she had left, the awful time that followed. I told her how mean Debbie had been and how jealous I felt of her, though I had tried and tried to conquer it. And how, at the same time, I hated being far away from her, that it seemed to be going on forever, and might be my fault. She listened in silence, only about half-way through she put out her gloved hand and held mine.

'I never expected to tell anyone,' I ended, rather shakily. 'Is it awful of me to be jealous? *She* can talk to anyone; you've seen what she's like at school. She's always gay, and she's so dazzlingly pretty, and she's going to be top of the class. She's going to be a ballerina, too, she's quite certain, and I-I'm not sure of anything.'

III

'Well,' said Mel forthrightly, 'one thing she *can't* be sure of is being a ballerina. We all know it will only be one in several hundred, or even one in several thousand. Just now she's only in a class of ordinary thirteen-year-olds, and—Does Miss Verney praise her dancing much?'

'No, that's a funny thing,' I said slowly. 'She doesn't seem to have said a word. But she doesn't criticize her much, either.' I paused, then added: 'She told *me* I'd been well taught and hadn't much to unlearn.'

Mel frowned.

'I'm not really the one to tell. P'rhaps I'm not old enough to give you good advice. But I think you're being a bit silly.' I jumped and she clutched my hand again. 'No, don't get shirty. I'll tell you what I mean. *I* don't think she's better looking than you, for a start.'

'But she *must* be. She's so striking, with all that silvery gold hair and her interesting pale face.'

'She's pretty, but so are you. You have lovely colouring, too. It was the first thing I noticed about you. Your hair is bright and your eyes are lovely, and you've got those rosy cheeks. And your face is a lot more thoughtful than hers; it has far more character.'

'Goodness!' I said, feeling very shy; embarrassed, really, but very comforted. No one had ever talked about my looks before.

'And then *is* she cleverer than you? Can't *you* be top of the class?'

'I was at school in Birkenhead, once or twice. I beat her because I *meant* to work. Only here she seems to have got into the new methods quicker and I thought perhaps it wasn't worth bothering.'

'Well, it jolly well is. I s'pose rivalry is awful, but my old dancing teacher says there's bound to be extra special rivalry in ballet schools. She hates it, but says it's quite inevitable. If I were you I'd work as hard as you can, and if you're top sometimes and Debbie's top others she can't really mind. If she does she not a nice person.'

'She's nice really,' I said defensively. 'It's only sometimes that she—that she—'

'Well, I'd get it out of your head that she's better at things than you. She may not even be a better dancer. Did anyone ever tell you so? Say so?'

'Only Debbie herself,' I confessed, feeling startled. 'But she did get higher marks in the exams, and I used to have a little trouble with my feet. It seems to be over now—'

'I bet all dancers have trouble with their feet some time in their lives. That's nothing, especially if it's gone.'

'But, Mel, you're forgetting the scholarship. *She* was given one and I—'

'Well, there *was* only one place. They had to give it to one of you. How do you know they didn't have a fierce argument as to which of you should have it?

It may not have been a foregone conclusion. Daft, you are. How could you tell? They offered you a place and then gave you the first chance of a scholarship.'

'But—perhaps because they wanted Debbie. That's the thing that—'

Mel snorted.

'You *are* daft, if you can believe that. What would be the good of them taking you if you were going to be a dead loss? Debbie wouldn't have balanced out, seems to me.'

'Oh, Mel, you *do* talk sense. I've been an idiot. I *will* work and try and believe in myself. Debbie has so much confidence.'

'Over-confidence, maybe,' Mel said sagely. 'She's very full of herself and no one seems to mind, I suppose because, as you say, she's always friendly and gay. Look here! We'll *both* work like anything. We always do at dancing and we'll go all out at lessons, too. We'll show 'em. Debbie isn't the only future ballerina. We've all got equal chances—'

'Not really. Don't you think that some people have the—the spark?'

Mel looked sober, tossing her pony-tail; when she moved the lights behind us shone on her thoughtful profile. I knew that she, too, sometimes felt doubts of the future.

'Perhaps they have, but we don't *know*. So we'll try and believe it might be us.'

'Yes,' I agreed fervently. Then: 'You've helped an

114

awful lot, Mel. But there's still the fact that Debbie and I don't seem to have any—any point of contact now.'

'Well, it's her fault, whether she knows it or not.'

'She *was* pretty horrid, and she isn't being very nice now. But I miss her very much, in a queer kind of way.'

'I should wait. Maybe she'll come round. Maybe something will happen. I quarrel with my sister sometimes. Once we didn't speak for a month.'

'But we never actually quarrelled, so it's harder to make it up. It's so—so subtle—'

The door behind us opened and Mrs Forrest's voice cried:

'Well, blimey! You kids still out here? Bin here twenty minutes. You'll catch your deaths and get me into trouble as well. Don't you want to come and see another view?'

We spun round and followed her into the light and warmth and the subject of Debbie and me wasn't mentioned again. But I felt ten times better and full of resolution. Mel was right, I had been silly to suffer so much. I was never going to let myself feel jealous or lacking in confidence again.

I was very grateful to Mel, for I was sure she really had talked sense. She seemed to me rather an unusual person and there was no doubt that she was clever. *She* was soon very near the top of the class.

When she was eleven she had passed to quite a

famous London day school and she had been there for two years before coming to the Lingeraux.

'We don't know where she gets her brains,' her mother said once, giving Mel a proud glance. 'We're ordinary folk, as you can see.'

They were, too, though very nice. I soon felt as though the overcrowded terrace house in Campden Town was a second home. Mel had an older sister, Cherry, and three brothers, and about the only thing that wasn't ordinary was their names. Cherry was Cherry Hinton Forrest, and the boys were Milton, Barton and Drayton, but always called Mill, Bartie and Dray. They were places near Cambridge, for Mrs Forrest had been born in the little village of Meldreth and had met her husband when she went to live and work in Portsmouth.

'Don't know what I should have done if I'd had another girl,' she said, laughing.

'You'd have called the poor child Cambridge, Mum,' said Mel.

Mr Forrest was usually away, but he was home for a few days early in February and Peter and I met him then. He was quite a good-looking man, with a nice smile, and he entertained us with stories of his experiences at sea.

Anyway, after that long talk with Mel I did begin to find things much easier at the Lingeraux. I continued to enjoy every moment of the ballet classes, and I liked the 'character' classes as well. At school lessons I worked harder than ever before and at the end of the second week in February I was second, with Mel top. Debbie was fourth and seemed surprised, but not really annoyed. She grinned and shrugged.

'I could work better if we didn't have to do our homework in that awful sitting-room.'

It wasn't really easy to work there, especially when Linda had the television on, but it was still far too cold for us to work upstairs. In fact it was bitter, with snowstorms every few days and a lot of frost. But the afternoons were growing much lighter, and sometimes Mel, Peter and I could snatch an hour to go exploring after school.

We had quite a varied life at the Lingeraux, for we were taken to concerts at the Royal Festival Hall, to the National Gallery and the Wallace Collection, and there were quite often lectures on a variety of subjects; the art of make-up, stage design, the history of dance and so on.

The man who gave the history of dance lecture was very famous indeed as a ballet critic and writer on the theatre and I had known his name for years. The whole school crowded into the hall and somehow I found Debbie next to me. She looked around and said:

'Such a lot of us! Do you know, sometimes I *hate* being one of a crowd. It makes me feel invisible.'

She had made quite a few remarks of that nature lately and I understand her well enough to know exactly how she was feeling. *I* was rather glad, just then, to be safely anonymous, but Debbie liked to stand out.

'You're far from invisible,' I said, thinking how pretty she looked. It really wasn't any good Mel telling me I was as nice-looking as Debbie. I thought it far more romantic to have fair hair and not much colour. She wasn't in the least insipid, because her eyes were so bright and her lips so red.

'I *mean* to be noticed,' said Debbie, in quite a low voice, so that her next door neighbour couldn't hear. 'My hopes are pinned on the Spring Show. They'll be starting to plan for it in March, Claudia says. It's held in the Lingeraux Theatre on the day we break up for Easter and there are always at least three ballets. One for the little ones, one for the middles and one for the boys and girls in Classes Five and Six. The senior students don't have anything to do with it. They have their own matinée before Christmas, when they do something grand like the whole of *Swan Lake*, with a few to help out from the Company.'

'But we haven't a hope of getting a part, even a small one,' I said, rather startled. I had already heard about the Spring Show, of course; *everyone* hoped for a chance to dance. It was the great event of the term, or even the year.

'Well, Claudia says they often give new students a chance. It's rather a policy of the School. And I simply don't see why *I* shouldn't get a part. I always danced the main rôle at the Grayland Show.'

Well, the Grayland wasn't the Lingeraux, as Debbie must really know very well, but her words gave me a sudden, springing hope. How *wonderful* if I could get a part, too, even if only a tiny one. Aunt Eileen and Linda could come and watch, and maybe Clyde. And to dance on the Lingeraux stage would be the most exciting thing that had ever happened.

Then I forgot all about Debbie beside me, and even, for the time being, the Spring Show, because the lecturer appeared on the platform and was introduced by Miss Sherwood. He was a very handsome man, tall and commanding, with a ringing voice. And of course I found every word that he said interesting. I knew quite a lot of it from my wide reading of ballet books and magazines, but some things were absolutely new to me.

Debbie was still near me when, after the lecture, we all streamed out into the entrance hall, and the great man was standing there talking to Miss Sherwood. We had been kept behind for a few minutes because the principal ballet mistress had something to say to us, and then we had to move our chairs to the side.

Debbie said in my ear:

'One way to get some notice would be to fall in a dead faint at his feet!'

'Oh, you wouldn't!' I gasped, not at all sure that she was joking.

'Well, I bet I could do it convincingly. And he'd

say: "Who is this beautiful young girl? So fair, so pale!" And maybe he'd write a piece about me for *Ballet Monthly*.'

'And maybe he'd say: "This one obviously isn't strong enough to be a dancer. Why on earth did you accept her?" ' I retorted tartly, and then saw that she was grinning mischievously. She went off with Claudia.

A few days later our class was taken to the Tate Gallery one afternoon. It was a dark, bitterly cold day and the wind swept icily off the river as we climbed out of the special bus on Millbank. The Tate loomed above us, very impressive, and I was thrilled, because I hadn't yet had a chance to go there and see the collection of French Impressionist and Post Impressionist paintings.

It was very exciting to go up the steps and into the entrance hall, which was very warm and bright. Beyond stretched the huge main hall, with modern sculptures here and there.

Miss Jacks, the art mistress, waited until we had left our coats in the cloakroom and then gave us a brief lecture on behaving well.

'Because' she said, 'a special exhibition is opening this afternoon in one of the rooms. Some important people will be there and I don't want the School disgraced if they chance to see any of us.' And she looked rather fixedly at the Russian boy, Serge, who was a bit of a clown. Surprising, I had thought it at first; I always believed Russians to be rather solemn and tragic.

She then led us from room to room, spending much too long on the Turners and Pre-Raphaelites, I thought. I was dying to get to the French rooms, and I particularly wanted to see the Utrillos. I knew they had his *Place du Tertre*, one of my favourite pictures.

We did get there in the end and I was very happy, not really listening to Miss Jacks, but taking my own pleasure in the paintings. Then she said that we were free to go and look again at any pictures we had liked particularly, and to meet by the main door in twenty minutes.

I stayed behind to look again at the four Utrillos and Debbie was there, too, for a time. Then gradually everyone wandered away. I followed them slowly, last of all to mount the stairs from the lower rooms, and the bigger rooms seemed very empty. Of course it was winter and a horrid day, so perhaps people hadn't been in the mood for making the journey to Millbank.

Eventually I wandered out into the long, tremendously high main hall. A little way away a smartly dressed party was emerging from the special exhibition and heading towards the exit. One man with a camera over his shoulder turned the other way and stood looking thoughtfully at a very peculiar piece of statuary.

I stood in the shadow of a pillar, thinking how

wonderful it was to have places like the Tate almost on our very doorstep, and how especially nice it was to see it almost empty, with no jostling crowd.

Then suddenly I saw Debbie near the far end of the hall. She was by herself; in fact there was no one else in sight from where I stood, except for the man with the camera, who had wandered in Debbie's direction, and a very bored-looking attendant who was standing just within a doorway on my left.

Debbie was walking slowly, almost on tip-toe, with her hands clasped behind her back, sometimes stopping to look at a piece of sculpture. I wondered why she had left her friends, but then Debbie really did like art and was far more knowledgeable than I was about sculpture. She had several pictures of famous sculptures in her postcard collection.

Debbie glanced vaguely up the hall, then unclasped her hands. She was almost dancing now . . . she *was* dancing. She suddenly did a series of pirouettes round the plinth on which the statue stood. She was wearing her Lingeraux suit and outdoor shoes, but somehow that didn't seem to matter. Her hair caught the light as she spun round. It seemed rather an odd thing to do, to turn pirouettes in the great hall of the Tate Gallery, yet I thought I knew how she felt. Such a lovely empty floor; so much space.

Then my heart leaped, for of course Debbie *shouldn't* dance in an art gallery. It might be against the law or something. My heart leaped even more when I saw the man stop looking vague and whip out his camera. He took a picture of the last pirouette and then walked quickly towards Debbie, who had her hands behind her back again, and was staring fixedly at a big block of stone.

'Debbie, you idiot!' I said to myself, starting towards her. But I was quite a long way away and the man had reached her. They were talking ... he had taken out a notebook and Debbie was smiling up at him, telling him something that he apparently wrote down.

Then he put the notebook away, said: 'Well, good-bye, kiddie. Thanks!' and strode away towards the exit, passing me without taking any notice of me. I rushed to Debbie's side.

'Did he take your picture? Oh, Debbie!'

Debbie grinned at my dismayed tone.

'Why so shocked?'

'But—But perhaps you shouldn't dance here and —and what's he going to do with the photograph?'

'Put it in his paper, I hope,' said Debbie cheer-fully, and just then Lotti and Claudia bore down on us.

'Come on, you two! Miss Jacks is waiting.'

I thought that that might be the end of it, so I didn't mention the odd little affair to anyone. But the next day when I got home from school Debbie was already there, with her nose in a London newspaper, and Aunt Eileen was crying:

'Well, I never! Just fancy that young man happening to see you dance! I must say it's a good picture. I asked Mrs Tonkings to buy a few more copies. You'll want to send one to your mother and dad.'

The picture really was awfully good. He had caught Debbie just as she whirled into sight round the statue. Underneath was printed: 'Young Dancer in the Tate Gallery. Miss Deborah Darke of the Lingeraux Ballet School dances a series of pirouettes in a most unusual place. Miss Darke is thirteen and came to London in September.'

Debbie was in bubbling spirits all evening.

'Well, at any rate I've come out of the crowd at last!' she said triumphantly.

When we arrived at school the next morning she was immediately besieged by her friends, most of whom had seen the picture.

'But when did you dance, Debbie? None of *us* saw you.'

They obviously thought she had done a very clever thing in getting her picture in the paper, but the school authorities took quite a different view. Debbie was sent for after the ballet class and remained in Miss Sherwood's room for some time. She looked rather subdued when she finally appeared in the classroom, but we couldn't question her until break. Then she said crossly:

'What a stuffy lot they are! I gave the school some nice publicity, I thought, but they aren't a bit grateful. In fact they're mad with me. Miss Jacks was there, too, and she seemed really annoyed. I wasn't doing any *harm*.'

'They are rather stuffy,' Claudia agreed. 'They won't let us accept any kind of professional engagement while we're here. It's not like a stage school, where kids get licences when they're twelve and go into pantomime and so on. All our parents had to sign that they agreed to the conditions.'

'I didn't know that,' said Debbie. 'But I don't suppose it matters.'

The affair didn't die down then because Debbie, amazingly, had several offers on the strength of that photograph. A film company offered her a test, a famous theatrical agent wanted to put her on his books, and a well-known management wanted her to audition for a West End play, in which they needed a young, fair girl.

All the offers had to be refused and Debbie was both thrilled and disgruntled. Then finally re-signed.

'What I really want,' she said, as we went to bed one night, 'is to be a ballerina, so I suppose I've got to stick to the Lingeraux and work hard for years and years. But gosh! I should have *loved* to try for films. And the play would have been fun, too.'

'And never be a dancer?' I said.

She frowned.

'I know. The Lingeraux would have turned me out. They made that quite clear.'

'How very, very strange it is that all this happened

just because you felt like dancing in the Tate. Such a coincidence that that photographer was there.'

Debbie stared at me. She was just ready to leap into bed. Her striped pyjamas were washed out and rather too small for her.

'Oh, Dorrie, you idiot!'

'Why?' I asked, puzzled.

'Well, dumb Dorrie Darke. I *knew* he was there, of course. I saw him much earlier, going into that special opening, and I spied him just as soon as he walked back into the hall. I *told* you I wasn't going to stay invisible.'

'Well,' I said to myself, 'I *am* dumb Dorrie Darke and no mistake.' Because I had never guessed.

* 10 *

The Spring Dance

On the whole the weeks of term passed very quickly and it seemed as though we had always been in London. Home seemed far away, and there were certainly still times when I missed it fiercely, but Easter would come and, meanwhile, life was terribly busy.

The evenings were much lighter, but there were not many signs of spring. Mel, Peter and I searched for buds in the parks, but there was nothing but a few spears of crocus, pushing up in the still frozen ground.

One Saturday the three of us went to Hampton Court, which I just loved, as the Tudor period had always interested me particularly and we were doing it in class just then, too. Another time we went to Epping Forest, but it was bitterly cold and bleak and we came home early.

'If only it were summer and we could lie in the sun!' I said wistfully. I did long for heat and blue skies.

At the Lingeraux, when March came, most of the

talk was about the coming Spring Show. Madame Lingeraux called the whole school together one afternoon (apart from the senior students) and told us about the different ballets. The junior one was to be a flower ballet, *The Magic Garden*, ours was to be one that had apparently been danced a couple of years before, *The Princess in the Secret Wood*, and the one for the older pupils *Moon in a Net*.

I listened breathlessly to the story of *The Princess*. It was about a Princess and her young lady-in-waiting, Amanda, who decided to go adventuring in the secret wood and all the things that happened to them there. The main part was, of course, the Princess, and Amanda had quite a lot of dancing, too. Then there were the Spirits of the Wood, the Green Witch, the Trees and quite a number of village children. The leader of the village children was called Betty and she had a very short solo dance.

'You see that there are a good many parts,' Madame Lingeraux said, smiling down at us from the stage. 'But even so only about one-third of the pupils will be able to dance. This, as I say every year, is quite inevitable, and I do ask you not to be too downcast if you aren't chosen. It need not be any reflection on your dancing. The lists will go up about the middle of the month, and from then onwards there will be intensive rehearsals, but we always try not to take too much time from your school lessons.'

Madame Lingeraux could talk until she was black

in the face, but of course every single boy and girl hoped for a part. One could see it in the bemused faces as we all dispersed.

'I do wish that Dad and Mother could come south to see me dance,' Debbie said that evening, looking up from her homework.

'To see *you* dance?' Aunt Eileen asked. 'I thought you didn't know yet who's going to get the parts.'

'Well, we don't. But somehow I feel it in my bones that I'll be chosen. I can't *imagine* not being chosen.'

'And what about Dorrie? What makes you think she won't be chosen, too?'

'Well, of course she may be. I didn't say she wouldn't. Only Dorrie has no push. She doesn't make people notice her.'

'She'll get along all right without that,' Aunt Eileen said tartly. 'It will just serve you right, Miss, if you get passed over.'

'I'll never be passed over,' said Debbie, with such calm certainty that, in a curious way, it wasn't really offensive. Oh, how I envied her that wonderful self-confidence!

Would I get a part? Oh, even a tree or the humblest village child would be enough, because it would mean being made-up in a real dressing-room and dancing on the Lingeraux stage. Debbie was quite right; I didn't push myself, but I seemed to have done well during the past few weeks. I had worked just as hard as I could, to the limit of my ability, and I was never very far from the top of the class at lessons. I felt all right in the ballet classes, too. My body seemed to obey me effortlessly and I was always happy. The constant repetition of those familiar exercises was no drudgery to me.

Just a little part . . . just any part. But in my imagination it didn't stop there. I began to day-dream about being chosen to dance the Princess, or at least Amanda, the young lady-in-waiting. Debbie would probably be the Princess, for she certainly looked the part. Well, Amanda would be lovely; Amanda in the secret wood, a wood that would, of course, only be painted scenery. Beyond the foot-lights would be the Lingeraux orchestra and then the blurred faces of the enraptured audience.

I could see us taking many calls at the end; the Princess, Amanda, and the handsome village youth, William, who rescued us from the clutches of the Green Witch. We would be given flowers, perhaps, and Dad and Mother would be there and would come behind afterwards to shower us with congratulations. I could actually hear Dad's voice saying:

'I'm proud of my ballet twins.'

Not that he would quite say that, of course. He had never called us his 'ballet twins'. It was the local newspaper that had used the term.

It didn't stop with day-dreaming. One night I dreamed that I was dancing the Princess on a stage far bigger than the Lingeraux one. It was a huge stage . . . Covent Garden, of course. And I wasn't, I suddenly realised, the Princess in that unimportant little children's ballet. I was Aurora in *The Sleeping Beauty*, and I was dancing the *Rose Adagio*. Each of the four Princes came to me in turn, as I balanced delicately *en pointe* . . . the music rose to that wonderful crescendo at the end. The applause rang out . . . the cheering . . . the wild thunder of clapping.

Then, of course, I awoke and it wasn't clapping, but the sound of Linda thumping on our door.

'Seven o'clock, kids! Rise and shine!'

But somehow the dream stayed with me and made me strangely, unexpectedly happy. I was, secretly, filled with almost as much confidence as Debbie, sure that I couldn't be passed over. Not the Princess, of course, maybe not even Amanda, but Madame had said that the Trees had a delightful little dance. I would settle joyfully for being a tree.

To add to my sudden flood of happiness and certainty of success, spring suddenly decided to show itself a little. There came a day, the thirteenth of March, when the sun was almost warm, and when we walked in Bloomsbury Square after lunch, the crocuses were making vivid pools of purple and gold in the beds. Even in London it seemed that one could smell spring in the air and it was intoxicating to feel the warm touch of the sun on my face.

We all went indoors somewhat reluctantly for afternoon school, and when I entered the class room Miss Lines asked me if I would take a message to Miss Verney, whom she thought was in the Green Studio with some of the senior students.

The Green Studio was one apart, reached by way of the big hall, and I went cheerfully, glad to have that much respite from lessons. The hall was quite empty and filled with sunlight, and suddenly I couldn't resist that lovely bare stretch of floor, for all the chairs were piled up at the sides.

I began to dance, and in an odd way I was suddenly possessed, inspired, as I had never been before. The memory of the sunlight and the crocuses and that nameless feeling of spring in the square all fused into movement. I think I had never been so happy in my life as I leaped and whirled, interpreting my feelings in conventional ballet movements and many that were not.

'The Spring Dance!' I thought. 'I'm a choreographer.' But mostly I didn't think at all, just let myself go to the faint music that was coming from the Green Studio. It was, I dimly realised, the rather wild, strange music that a modern composer had created for one of Madame Lingeraux's ballets.

It was glorious while it lasted, but suddenly the mood was gone and I remembered the message and the fact that someone might come in at any moment. I tried to tidy my hair with my hand, and, a little breathless, opened the studio door. Miss Verney didn't notice me at once, so I was able to watch the six senior students for a few moments. It must be wonderful to be a senior student, I thought; it meant that admission to the Company was almost certain, and, even while still in the School, they had walk-on parts or even filled in if the *corps de ballet* needed a few extra members.

When I returned to the hall Madame Lingeraux herself was standing in the middle of the floor, apparently lost in thought. Though she had been nice to me the very few times I had had contact with her I was still, in company with most people, very much in awe of her. I tried to get past her with only a mumbled 'Good afternoon, Madame!', but she fixed me with her bright, almost black eyes and said:

'And how are *you* these days? Settled down, have you?'

'I—I think so, thank you, Madame.'

'You've a good colour, not like some of these pasty London children.'

I could feel my face immediately flaming, so that my colour was greatly improved.

'I—I often wish I were pale and interesting.'

She cackled at that, rather alarmingly. She often looked and sounded a bit like a witch, a plump witch.

'You wouldn't like it if you were anaemic. It can be a perfect nuisance and not at all interesting. Well, get along, child. Oughtn't you to be working? I suppose you're as idle as the rest of them.'

'Idle!' I said to myself, as I dashed away. 'None of us get the chance to be idle in this school.'

I hoped very much that she didn't really believe I was lazy. I wondered if she ever saw the class lists, or was that only Miss Sherwood's business? Yet

133

people said that Madame had a finger on every aspect of the School and I was fully prepared to believe it.

Excitement mounted and mounted, as the days passed. The lists for the Spring Show might go up any day, any hour. Even people like Claudia or Serge, who had been at the Lingeraux for quite a long time, were restless and unsettled, and everyone made excuses to walk past the big notice-board in the entrance hall. But the fourteenth of March passed and nothing had happened.

'It will be today,' said Lotti, the next morning. 'I know it will be today.'

And my spine tingled with excitement and dread. Oh, just a tree, if I couldn't be Amanda! I must, must, must get something. I didn't know how I would live if I were left out.

Lunch was delayed that day owing to some mishap in the kitchen and by the time we were drinking our milky coffee it was almost time for the bell to ring for afternoon school. Suddenly a very small junior dashed into the canteen.

'I say, everyone! The lists are up! The lists are up!' she cried.

Peter knocked over his cup, but fortunately there wasn't much in it. Debbie, Lottie and Claudia had already gone and the others were following quickly. Mel said:

'Are you coming. Dorrie?'

'In a minute,' I said, trying to make my voice

sound calm. 'You and Peter go on. I'll—just finish this.'

Mel and Peter gave me understanding looks and went away, and I finished my coffee—pretty nasty it was, at the best of times—and rose slowly. I *couldn't* hurry. Suddenly I knew that I couldn't see those lists in the company of all the others. Not even, really, with Mel and Peter.

So I went along to the cloakroom and washed my hands and combed my hair. The looking-glass was spotted with damp and it was a constant joke that it made one look terrible. I certainly looked most unusually pale and I felt sick. But it was mostly excitement. I was fairly sure that it would be all right, that I would have got something.

Finally, still very slowly, I went up the stairs. The bell had gone a few moments before and by the time I neared the top of the stairs the hall was almost empty. Mel and Peter were just being ordered up the stairs by one of the big girls.

I ducked back until everyone had gone. My friends had obviously wanted to wait. They must know I hadn't seen the lists yet. And if I didn't hurry I'd be in trouble over being late for class.

I took a deep breath and walked across the hall towards the notice-board.

✳ 11 ✳

Dorrie Alone

It was always rather dark in the hall, even when the sun was shining, and at first I couldn't clearly see the various lists and notices that hung on the board. Then I found them on the right-hand side. There was a special strip heading, saying 'Spring Show', and then three separate lists.

I ignored *The Magic Garden* and *Moon in a Net*, for they couldn't possibly concern me. The only ballet that mattered was *The Princess in the Secret Wood*. My hands felt damp and I could hear my heart thudding.

The Princess in the Secret Wood! Claudia was the Princess, a girl called Caroline Best from the class below was Amanda ... Serge was William, the village youth ... Lotti the Green Witch. Debbie was Betty, the leader of the village children.

My heart was thudding louder than ever and I could hardly breathe. I blinked to try and clear my sight. I looked down the rest of the list, right to the bottom of the Trees, but my name was not there.

At first I couldn't believe it. My happiness and certainty must have gone quite deep, because it was the most appalling shock. I had worked so hard, hoped so much, and I had got nothing. I wasn't even the humblest tree or village child.

I didn't know what to do or where to go to be alone. I *couldn't* go upstairs as though nothing had happened and face their possible pity and commiseration. Debbie would be so thrilled at being chosen to be Betty, for she would have that little solo dance. It wasn't the Princess, but it was quite a lot, all the same, for a new girl. Mel and Peter, I had dimly noticed, were both trees.

No, I couldn't face it. I couldn't bear it. I had to get away. It wasn't even any good hiding in the cloakroom, because I would probably be discovered.

I don't really think my mind was working at all clearly. I only had that overpowering urge to get away, to be alone to face my desperate diappointment.

I bolted down to the cloakroom, and, with fumbling, ice-cold fingers (though it was warm down there), I put on my coat, beret and scarf, changed my shoes. Then, taking my case, I went upstairs again, not even trying to be cautious, but there was still no one at all about in the hall. It was silent and offered escape. The front door was not far away.

I pulled it open and heard it shut with a snap behind me. I almost fell down the steps.

The springlike weather had lasted. It was sunny and almost warm out of doors, but I scarcely noticed. I turned north and soon came to Russell

Square, then Woburn Square ... Gordon Square. It helped me just to keep moving, but I nearly got run over on more than one occasion.

I hopped out of the way of a swooping taxi in Gordon Square and the driver leaned out to swear at me. But I crossed Euston Road safely. I never thought at all about what I was doing ... that I had simply walked out of the Lingeraux and might get into trouble. I only wanted to get away, preferably out of London. I had a desperate, only half-formed need for open spaces.

I plunged down into the Tube at Euston and, almost at random, took a ticket for Highgate. Mel, Peter and I had been there one Saturday afternoon and walked to Ken Wood House. It was lucky that I had some money with me; Dad had sent us both postal orders for five shillings only the day before and I still had most of it left.

The train roared and rattled northwards and still I didn't think. Once or twice tears welled up in my eyes and I blinked them back fiercely, because I couldn't cry in public. I thought if I once started I should never stop. I must have looked a little strange, for a fat, motherly woman suddenly leaned forward and asked:

'Are you all right, dear?'

I nodded and said, 'Yes, thank you.' I didn't want her sympathy, *any* sympathy. I was much relieved when she left the train at Archway.

It was better in Highgate. I walked very fast along

quiet, sometimes tree-arched streets. There were big, peaceful houses and the sound of bird-song. The smell of earth and the soft blaze of crocuses reminded me forcibly of my joy on that day when I had danced. Only two days ago! I couldn't bear to think about it and I walked even faster. I couldn't cry in Highgate, either, for there were a few people about.

Presently I reached Ken Wood House, but I didn't go into the building. I cut away across the gardens and into the woods. It was very quiet there and I met almost no one. The paths were a little muddy, but I found a dry and secret corner and flung myself down on some old leaves. And then I *did* cry, for a long, long time.

I am almost ashamed to have to explain all this, but it is part of the story and has to be told. I cried and sobbed and shook, burrowing down into the leaves. Madame Lingeraux, as I remembered even in the midst of my shame and disappointment, had expressly said that we weren't to mind if we weren't chosen. She had said that only about a third of the pupils in the school could hope to be in the ballets. I was not the only one to be left out.

But other people didn't have a sister called Debbie, or know how awful it was to be the one who always came second. *Debbie* would dance on the Lingeraux stage; Aunt Eileen, Linda and maybe Clyde would go to watch her, and I would only be in the audience, playing second fiddle as always.

It wouldn't have mattered nearly as much if I

hadn't worked so hard, and if I hadn't felt so much unusual hope and confidence.

I cried until I was exhausted and then I realized that the leaves were damp, after all. I'd probably get rheumatism if I stayed there. So I mopped myself up as best I could, horrified by the look of my face in the little mirror in the lid of my case. I brushed my coat, straightened my stockings and set off again.

I wandered for a long time, somewhere on Hampstead Heath. There was still almost no one about and gradually the sunny silence, the suggestion of green buds in hollows, soothed and comforted me. At last I began to think more coherently, and it was then that shame really started. For of course I had definitely done something awful when I ran away from school like a baby. I was sure to be missed and everyone would know why I had gone.

It had been a cowardly, stupid thing to do and I would never live it down. I should probably go down in the annals of the Lingeraux School as the girl who ran away because she didn't get a part in the Spring Show.

Debbie would laugh at me, perhaps, and Aunt Eileen would be angry. Or she might very well be worried as well. Perhaps, when I was discovered to be missing, they would telephone her. She and everyone would soon know that Doria Drake was a spineless girl, with not enough character to face up to a disappointing situation. I suddenly heard Mel's voice saying, 'Your face has far more character.'

Well, she had been wrong. Spineless, soggy, feeble Dorrie Darke.

I sat down again under a gorse bush and tried to think, that time really constructively.

It had happened; I hadn't been chosen and I had run away. Nothing could wipe out either of those facts. So somehow I had to set my chin and face the thing. I had to go back to the Lingeraux . . . But not that day. A glance at my watch, the first time I had looked at it, told me that it was already nearly four o'clock. And I was somewhere in the heart of Hampstead Heath, not even on a main path. I hadn't the remotest idea where I was, in fact. Earlier I had been able to hear distant traffic, but now all I could hear was an aeroplane somewhere far overhead.

Aunt Eileen would be horrified if she could see me. She was always rather nervous about us and often prophesied dire things. 'Doomisms', naturally, but she would have thought it most dangerous for me to be in the middle of the Heath alone. Not that there seemed to be any danger. There wasn't a soul anywhere. It might have been the heart of the real country.

All right, so I had missed the whole afternoon at school. I was certainly in trouble, but I would have to face it. And of course it wasn't the end of the world because I wasn't in the ballet. There would be other Spring Shows, and I had no choice but to go on working and hoping. Not unless I wanted to give up all idea of being a dancer, and that was unthinkable.

I suddenly saw my behaviour as absolutely silly as well as shameful. The fact that I had acted on the spur of the moment, entirely without conscious thought, was no excuse at all. In an obscure way it made it worse.

I got up again and began to walk rapidly out of the hollow where I had been sitting. The path was narrow and uneven and I was walking very fast. Suddenly I tripped over a stone and wrenched my ankle so painfully that for a moment everything went black.

I sank down again and waited for the agony to pass, which eventually it did, but walking was painful and difficult. I heard children's voices in the distance and even thought of calling for help. But what could they do? They couldn't carry me to the nearest bus stop or Tube station.

I could hear traffic now and suddenly, to my great relief, I emerged on to a broad path. There were quite a lot of people in sight and, when I struggled up the rise, I could see buildings to the left and a red London bus passing along a road quite near. It really was a tremendous relief, as it was by then after five o'clock and all I really wanted was to get to a telephone.

On the road I asked a passing woman if I was near a Tube station and she told me that Hampstead Station wasn't far away.

But first a telephone. . . . When I found a booth I had to wait for five awful minutes while a woman

chatted to a friend. I could hear snatches of her conversation when there wasn't too much traffic and it
seemed dreadfully trivial.

I must have looked desperate, for eventually she
opened the door and asked:

'You want to come in, ducks?'

'Please! It's terribly urgent,' I said. So then she
talked for another minute or two and hung up.

I already had the money in my hand and I wasted
no time. Aunt Eileen's voice spoke almost at once
and I gasped with relief.

'Hullo! Who is it? Dorrie? Is it you, dear? Speak
up; I can't hear you!'

'I—I—I—Aunt Eileen, I'm at Hampstead.'

'At *Hampstead*? What on earth are you doing
there? I've been frantic with worry. They rang up at
two-thirty from the Lingeraux to ask if you were here,
and of course you weren't. And I've been having
visions of every sort of terrible thing. I was just going
to telephone the police—'

'Oh, don't! I'm all right, honestly. I—I'm sorry. I
ran away. I know now that I was silly.'

'Ran away? Why? Debbie says she knows of
nothing that could have upset you. Well, listen . . .
Just where are you in Hampstead?'

'Not far from the Tube station and I've got money.
I'll be back as quickly as I can. And, Aunt Eileen,
I—I'm terribly sorry.'

'I shan't have an easy moment until you're back,'
she said. 'The rush hour, too . . . still it'll be going

the other way. Except that most probably you won't be able to get on a bus at Euston. Listen, Dorrie, are you still there?'

'Yes,' I said faintly. If I couldn't get on a bus I was going to have to walk, and my ankle still ached. I might really damage it.

'Take a taxi when you get to Euston. You sound done in. Tell the man I'll pay when you get here.'

'Yes, all right,' I said.

It was wonderful to be on the way home, but when at last I sat in the taxi, being driven rather slowly in the rush hour traffic down Gower Street, I wasn't looking forward to my reception. To facing Debbie . . . to facing the whole result of my behaviour. But I had to and I was going to. I was going to explain honestly, and apologise to everyone, and never be such a fool again. Only it really was awful of Debbie to say she didn't know why I had been upset; I couldn't understand that.

I could see faces at the upper windows of the house when the taxi stopped, so the students must know all about it. Aunt Eileen and Debbie were on the doorstep, and Debbie's eyes were red, as I noticed with amazement. She couldn't have been *crying*! Debbie, who never cried.

Aunt Eileen paid the man, then led me indoors, making clucking noises.

'Child, you look terrible! Your face . . . your coat! What are all those marks on the back of your coat?

Your face is filthy and you look. . . . Have you hurt yourself?'

'Only my ankle a bit. I ricked it. I—I'm all right.'

'You don't look it. Get your things off and I'll just telephone Madame Lingeraux to tell her you're here. I rang after I'd spoken to you, and she seemed much relieved, but she asked me to let her know when you got here. You're shivering, child. It's gone cold. Keep close to the fire.'

'M-Madame!' I stammered, in horror. 'Oh, does *she* know? Is she mad with me?'

'Of course she knows. They told her, naturally. I expect she is angry with you; who wouldn't be? But she was worried, too, None of us understands what happened; why you ran away.' She was dialling the number as she spoke.

'Madame Lingeraux?' she said, into the telephone. 'She's here. Says she's ricked her ankle and she looks all in. No, I haven't had time to get anything out of her. I will, yes. I'll ask my own doctor to look at her foot. In the morning, yes, if she's able to go to school. I'll tell her.'

'Oh, dear! Oh, how awful!' I thought, as the blessed warmth of the fire began to reach me. Debbie stood on one foot near by; silent and oddly sub-dued.

Aunt Eileen hung up and then turned to me.

'You must have a hot drink at once. Your tea's ready. So get your coat off and never mind anything else for the moment. Debbie, where are her slippers?

Her ankle *is* quite puffy. Everything else can wait till afterwards.'

It was nice to be fussed over, but I wasn't looking forward to 'afterwards'. I was just dreading it.

Debbie and Dorrie

I was going to argue that I couldn't eat a thing, though I longed for a cup of tea, but the moment Aunt Eileen put a plate of food in front of me I knew that I was ravenous, in spite of what might come afterwards.

'Get on with your homework, Debbie.' Aunt Eileen said, in the kind of tone one couldn't ignore. Debbie gave us both doubtful glances and then, without a word, moved to the cleared space at the end of the table, took out her books and began, very slowly, to write.

Aunt Eileen then went back to the telephone and called the doctor.

'I'd be glad if you'd look at her foot, Dr Thompson. A dancer you know; can't have anything wrong with it. Yes, at the end of surgery. Thank you.' Then she turned back to me. 'You can leave your homework tonight, Dorrie. You don't look in any shape to tackle it.'

'But—But I ought—I must—'

'Finish your tea,' she ordered, and I obeyed, but by

the end of it, though feeling better physically, I was boiling up into really awful anxiety. I pushed the plates aside and looked at her desperately.

'But are they really terribly mad with me? Is Madame?'

'Well, you can't expect them to be delighted when you gave everyone a most anxious afternoon. I should think that girls have been expelled for less, you silly child. Anyway, if the doctor'll let you go, you'll have to face Madame at ten o'clock tomorrow morning. In her office.'

'Oh, *no*!' I groaned, dreadfully frightened. Miss Sherwood wouldn't have been half as bad.

Aunt Eileen gave me a look in which pity and annoyance were mingled.

'Well, come and sit by the fire and put that foot up on the buffet. The doctor won't be here for some time yet and by then you'd better be in bed. Best place for you. Debbie's lit the fire, so it'll be warm up there. Now, Miss, let's have the whole story. What on earth possessed you to behave in that stupid way? Debbie says that the last she saw of you you were sitting in the canteen with your friends and apparently perfectly all right. So—'

'I was all right then,' I said, in a muffled voice. But I had made up my mind to face it all bravely, so I gulped and went on: 'That was before I saw the lists—the lists for the Spring Show, you know. I'd worked so hard and h-hoped so much, and then, when I didn't get a part, not even a tiny one, I—I just had to get away. I know now it was an awful thing to do. I knew it about half-way through the afternoon, but then it was too late.'

Just then Linda came in, ready for her evening date. She said in her usual breezy way:

'I saw the return of the prodigal from my window. Are you all right, Dorrie? What got you?'

'She's all right and we're talking,' Aunt Eileen said, still in that tone that brooked no nonsense. Linda flashed me a commiserating look and shrugged.

'O.K., I'll make myself scarce. I think I hear Derek, anyway. 'Bye, everyone! You'll survive, Dorrie.' And she was gone to open the front door.

During this exchange Debbie had pushed back her books and was staring at me with wide, startled eyes.

'Didn't get a part?' she said now. 'But—'

'But Debbie said—' Aunt Eileen began, looking bewildered.

'I looked at the list for *The Princess in the Secret Wood* and my name wasn't there. I saw that Debbie was Betty and—and so I ran away. I *know* I was childish. I know—'

'Dorrie, will you listen?' Debbie almost shouted. '*You* are Betty, you silly, great, lunatic chump!'

'*Debbie!*'

'Well, Aunt Eileen, she is. A daft, idiotic—'

'Debbie, if you can only call your sister names please be quiet.'

'I *know* it said "Betty, Deborah Darke",' I said, staring at both of them. My heart was leaping and I was wishing I hadn't eaten all those sausages.

'It said "Betty, D. Darke",' Debbie told me.

'But—But—Well, that must have been you. There weren't *two* Darkes down.' I was still gasping. 'You *can't* mean you didn't get a part?' I added faintly. I couldn't believe any of it.

'Oh, I got one. Of course I did. If you'd looked at the other lists you'd have seen. I'm the New Moon in *Moon in a Net*. It's quite a small rôle—the Full Moon is the chief one—but I do get a tiny solo dance. It said "Deborah Darke" on *that* list, so I suppose the secretary thought "D. Darke" was enough for the other one, though it was rather careless of her. When Claudia, Lotti and I went up to look Miss Verney was there, and she explained that they needed someone young and very fair for the New Moon and it was better to have me than someone in a wig. She asked if I minded very much not being in our own ballet, and of course I don't, so long as I'm in something. None of us *dreamed* you'd read it wrongly. I thought you'd be quite thrilled to get Betty. And—And—It was all so awful, and now you've made everyone mad, you idiot, and—'

I sank down into silence. *I* had been chosen to be Betty, and Debbie was quite right. I'd made everyone angry as well as worried, and Madame would almost certainly say that a girl who behaved so badly must be deprived of her part as a punishment.

Aunt Eileen glanced at me quickly and said:

'Well, I suppose it will work out somehow. It's all been most unfortunate, and I must say you were rather silly, Dorrie. Get upstairs now and have a hot bath. Go with her, Debbie, and see she's all right. I'll have to get on with the students' supper.'

I dragged myself weakly up the first flight of stairs. My ankle didn't feel too bad, it had almost stopped hurting, but my knees felt wobbly. Debbie hovered anxiously behind.

'Are you all right? Shall I ask someone to help?'

'No, I'm all right. I—I must just go slowly.'

Clyde's door opened as we gained the first landing.

'Well, hi! You're back O.K. What's the matter?'

'She's hurt her ankle,' said Debbie.

'Well, I guess I can manage to carry you to the top.'

'No, you can't. I'm heavy,' I protested.

'Heavy! A little slim girl like you? Mean to say you think I'm a weakling?' And he seized me in his arms and carried me firmly up the remaining flights. Rachel and Sara both came out to see what was happening.

'What's up with her? Can we help? Where did you get to, Dorrie?'

'She's fine. Just tired and hurt her foot a little.'

'She's going to have a bath and go to bed,' said Debbie, still close behind.

'Well, we'll come and see you later. Was Mrs Doom mad?'

151

'Not very p-pleased,' I said.

Debbie went down again to run the hot water in the bathroom on the floor below and Clyde dumped me gently on my bed.

'O.K. now? Shall I come back and carry you down when you've got your robe on?'

'No, thank you. I can manage all right,' I told him, and he said:

'Well, cheer up, kid. You're home all in one piece.' Then he went away and I undressed, put on my dressing-gown and slippers and went slowly down into a comforting cloud of steam. I *was* home all in one piece, but that was about all. My thoughts were still whirling. Oh, what had I done? What was going to happen to me at the Lingeraux *now*? Betty, oh, Betty! I had been given Betty when Mel was only a tree. And now I was going to lose it.

Debbie seated herself on the stool and surveyed me through the steam. She looked rather odd still, though her eyes had almost stopped being red. For some reason I felt quite shy with her, but I soon began to relax in the lovely hot water. It felt wonderful, only—

'Oh, I have made a mess of things!' I wailed.

'You certainly have,' Debbie retorted, in more her usual tone. Then she said in a burst: 'Oh, Dorrie, I'm so *glad* you're back safely! You've no idea how awful it was. Everyone questioning me, as though I'd murdered you and hidden the body. Even Madame. She was in the building, and they told her, and she asked to see me. . . . I was shattered. And then, when I came h-home, Aunt Eileen started dreadful Doomisms and I was sure you'd never be found again. Or only your d-dead body. And then I knew—well, I'd have missed—I couldn't imagine life without you.'

'Goodness!' I cried, genuinely astonished and then moved. This was Debbie come back, not the rather hard and remote sister I had known for so long.

'Why "goodness"? We're twins, aren't we? You don't think I want a *dead* twin, do you?'

'I don't know what you want,' I said slowly. 'You have so many friends, and you haven't been a bit nice—'

'Well, neither have you. You've seemed a thousand miles away for a long time. There didn't seem anything I could do, so I didn't try. Just let you go your own way.'

'You mean you think that I—I haven't been n-nice?'

'Well, have you? You didn't talk, and you seemed to disapprove of me. I didn't know what I'd *done*—'

The steam was clearing and I stared at her as though I had never seen her before. She didn't understand. She didn't know what she'd done. I think I realised then that Debbie just wasn't sensitive and I would have to come to terms with the fact. She wouldn't change.

'But, Debbie, don't you remember? It all started during that awful week-end in September. You were so horrid, and then, when they gave me a scholarship after all, you said—'

Debbie gaped at me.

'You mean you still hold that against me? I say a lot of things I don't mean. My reckless tongue. But it wasn't important. I can't even remember a word of what I said. I was just cross and disappointed—'

'Yes, I see,' I said slowly, tenderly soaping my slightly puffy ankle. 'But didn't you think I might be hurt? I was minding awfully badly about everything.'

'But so was I. We were both in a jam. You *can't* hold that against me, it wouldn't be reasonable. Let's be jolly again, Dor. Let's be as we used to be.'

'All right,' I agreed, and she heaved a big sigh of relief.

'Well, *that's* all right, anyway. One thing out of the way. We've still got Madame to worry about, and Betty—'

'Yes.' I didn't want to stay in the bath any longer. I felt sick with regret for the loss of Betty. For I was convinced that I was going to lose that part.

Soon after I was in bed Aunt Eileen came up with the doctor, who was quite young and very nice. He examined my ankle, took my temperature and said:

'Not very much wrong with her. Tired and upset, that's all. A good night's sleep will put most of that right. The ankle . . . well, I'm going to put an elastic bandage on it, just for extra support. She ought to stay off it as much as possible for day or two. Certainly no dancing. If she stays in bed tomorrow—'

'Oh, doctor, I can't! Honestly I can't! I'm in trouble and I've got to go to school and face it. I shall *die* if I'm stuck here!'

'The Lingeraux?' he said. 'Not far, is it? Well, I suppose you won't do yourself much good if you lie here worrying. Go to school then, but don't move about any more than necessary, and go straight to bed when you come home,'

'Oh, thank you!' *Anything* was better than staying at home with my thoughts.

'I'll give you a note for the school. They'll probably want their own doctor to look at your foot. Not that it's much to worry about.'

No, there were worse things. I lay alone and squirmed, while Debbie finished her homework below. Yet there was a small core of inner peace, because Debbie and I might be happier together in future. I still felt that there was quite a lot of thinking to do on that score, but not just at the moment.

I was glad when Sara came bouncing up after supper. She brought me the latest Terence Rattigan play and some peppermints, and stayed to chatter about her day at R.A.D.A. She didn't ask any questions about my escapade and I was grateful. Sara had scarcely gone when Rachel came in, bringing some chocolate and a pile of magazines. She was very happy, because she had got her boy friend back.

'I don't really think he's much good, Dorrie. He's too much of a ditherer. But I *did* miss him, and at least it means I can't be as unattractive as I thought.'

Rachel was still there when Clyde arrived with a box of candy, followed closely by Winston Marshall with more sweets and magazines. Then came Arthur Moorhead with nothing, but being kind enough to want to know how I was, and finally Melinda arrived with a bunch of violets, which we put in my tooth-glass. They all sat on Debbie's bed and Aunt Eileen looked rather scandalised when she came up to see how I was.

'My goodness! Gentlemen in your bedroom, Dorrie!' But she smiled at all of them. 'She's a lucky girl to have so many good friends, but I think you'd better go now. She must have plenty of sleep, if she really means to go to school tomorrow.' When they had departed she went on: 'Two of your friends telephoned; Mel and Peter. Mel seemed really upset. I said you were home and quite all right and that they might see you in the morning.'

I didn't sleep much. After Debbie came up we talked for quite a long time, and even when I settled down my thoughts were whirling so much that I couldn't relax. I couldn't forget that I had to face Madame at ten o'clock the next morning. I couldn't forget that I might lose Betty, and now I longed more violently than ever to dance on the Lingeraux stage.

About two o'clock I went cold all over, wondering

if the very worst would happen and they would ask me to leave. About four I fell into an exhausted sleep, from which Linda's usual thumping on the door awakened me.

* 13 *

Facing Madame Lingeraux

Needless to say I didn't feel too good, but I was determined to go to school. Aunt Eileen shook her head and said I was a silly girl not to stay in bed, but, after eating the minimum of breakfast, I set off with Debbie. Debbie was being her very nicest, which was some comfort, but nothing could alter the fact that I had to face Madame as well as all the rest.

Mel and Peter were just crossing the square as we approached and they turned and saw us, then came running back.

'Oh, *Dorrie*, you've come!' Mel cried. 'Your aunt said last night that you might, if your ankle wasn't too bad.'

'We're right glad to see you,' said Peter, beaming at me.

Debbie tactfully melted away, and I was left with my friends on either side of me, both looking at me rather anxiously. Of course they probably knew nothing beyond the fact that I had run away and hurt my foot.

As we approached the school I told them a little.

'I *know* I was a fool and a coward, but I really did think it was Debbie who was Betty. Mel understands; you don't, quite, Peter. But Debbie always seems to come first, and I—I thought she had again, that I'd got nothing. And now I have to face Madame, and she'll be mad, and I shan't be able to keep Betty.'

'Oh, I do hope you can keep her!' cried Mel, very generously, because she would probably have loved to dance Betty herself.

'I may even be expelled.'

'Oh, they wouldn't do that. Don't be daft, lass. Not just for missing afternoon school,' Peter protested, his nice face very troubled.

'And upsetting everyone and wasting their time. They may think I'm not a stable type—'

'Maybe they'll put it down to your artistic temperament,' Mel suggested hopefully.

'Are we allowed to have one, at thirteen? They're much more likely to think it was just sheer naughtiness. Oh, I wish I'd stayed in bed today, as the doctor wanted,' I groaned.

It was pretty awful meeting all the others, because they did stare at me, and several asked if I was all right. Most of them were nice to me, really, and not inquisitive, and Claudia even came up especially to say:

'Debbie says you've got to see Madame. Don't be too scared. She isn't so bad, really. She'll understand.'

But I couldn't imagine *explaining* to Madame. I thought I should be completely tongue-tied and that would make everything worse.

I didn't have to change, of course, as I wasn't to dance, but I went along to the studio and gave the doctor's note to Miss Verney. She asked about my ankle and said she would pass the note on to Miss Sherwood. The school doctor would be in later to see one of the juniors and could have a look at my foot.

She didn't ask any questions, or seem angry with me, but I felt wretched as I trailed upstairs to the classroom. It was quite empty and I knew that I should try to do some of my untouched homework, but I couldn't settle down. I walked round the big room, looking at the modern reproductions on the walls, then stood at the window, looking out across Bloomsbury Square. It wasn't a very nice day, rather grey and blustery, but the crocuses were still bright.

My stomach was behaving strangely and I felt cold, in spite of the central heating. I wished that it were ten o'clock, so that I could get the dreaded interview over. Yet the other side of me would have given anything to avoid it.

About twenty-five past nine I sat down at my desk and opened my books, and it was just as well because Miss Lines came in. She went briskly to her desk, then turned and saw me.

'Oh, you're there, Dorrie? Someone said you'd hurt your foot.'

'It's not much, Miss Lines. Just—Just ricked a bit.'

I felt bad enough facing her, but to my amazement she didn't ask any questions either. She just smiled at me and said:

'Well, I suppose you've some work to get on with?'

'Yes. I—I didn't do my homework last night. I—I've to see Madame at ten.'

She merely nodded and absorbed herself in some books she took out of her case.

It was twenty to ten, a quarter to. . . . I heard footsteps and voices below as everyone began to come out of the ballet classes. Just after five to ten the members of my class began to troop in and I put away my books and rose. I felt so terrible that I thought I might be sick on the way to Madame's office.

I met Mel in the corridor and she took one look at my probably white face and said:

'Oh, Dorrie, it's rotten! I'm so sorry. But she may be all right.'

'I'm scared to death of her,' I answered. My lips felt stiff and my teeth actually chattered as I went downstairs. It was just no good telling myself that Madame had always been quite nice to me. She wouldn't be nice now, when I had behaved so badly.

I half-expected that Miss Sherwood, the principal ballet mistress and perhaps half a dozen other august people would be there, but when I knocked and timidly opened the office door Madame was alone, writing at her desk. She looked up briefly, said: 'Good morning, Doria. Sit down, will you?' and continued to write.

I sat down on the edge of a chair facing her, wishing wildly that I had gone and been sick while I had the chance. The office was rather well furnished, with a thick grey carpet. If I were sick on that carpet that would just put paid to everything.

Madame Lingeraux looked to me much more formidable than usual. Small and fat she might be, but she couldn't have looked more awe-inspiring if she had been ten feet high. I jumped and nearly fell off the chair when she looked up. The bright black eyes surveyed me and then she put out her hand to the telephone. I thought that she was going to send for Miss Sherwood. but, amazingly, she asked for the canteen and then said:

'Madame Lingeraux speaking. Send me up a pot of *strong* coffee, please. Really strong, not that dishwater you give the students. And two cups.'

She replaced the receiver and said to me: 'You look as though you need it.'

'M-Madame,' I stuttered desperately, 'I think I'm going to be s-sick on the carpet.' It felt like a nightmare.

'Rubbish!' she said promptly. 'Don't you dare! What's there to be sick about? Go and sit in that other chair. It's more comfortable, so relax that tense stomach. How's the foot this morning?'

'Oh, it's nearly—nearly all right.' I practically fell into the lower chair. 'But—'

'I want to hear the whole story, of course. You must have had a reason for running away in that precipitate fashion. Someone unkind to you?'

'Oh, *no*, Madame!'

'Well, that's good. We don't get much unkindness here, but I suppose one never knows. Your sister said she could think of no reason for your being upset.'

'D-Debbie didn't know.'

The coffee came then, brought by a girl from the canteen. Madame poured out two cups and handed one to me.

'Put it on that little table and stop shaking, child. Take plenty of sugar. Now drink some.' I obeyed, burning my throat, but it was wonderful coffee. Quite different from our 'dishwater'. It made me feel better almost at once.

'Now let me hear your story.'

I looked at her helplessly. She just didn't talk like a famous figure, someone who was often in the limelight. Why, only the other day she had been on television.

'Something to do with that twin of yours, was it?'

And then I started to talk. I had never, never imagined telling Madame, but gradually I told her the same story that I had told Mel, only of course adding the end part. How I had though it was Debbie who was Betty and all the rest, including the way I had realised that, even without a part, I must face the situation.

'And—And I've had such a terrible night, thinking I was going to be expelled, or of course lose Betty—'

Madame Lingeraux silently poured second cups of coffee and handed mine back to me. My hand had stopped shaking, that was something. Then she said, in quite a gentle voice:

'I see. I thought it might be something like that, though none of us realised about the "D. Darke". You really saw it as Deborah?'

'I—well, I suppose I must have done. It seems silly now. But even if—I would still have thought that "D. Darke" was Debbie.'

'Well, your friend Mel seems to have talked sense to you and there's not much I can add, except to tell you straight from the horse's mouth—' and she gave her characteristic cackle—'that *I* wanted you to have the scholarship. There wasn't much in it, but I look for character as well as for good technique.'

'You wanted *me*?'

'Yes. As I say, there was very little in it and we had to give the scholarship to one of you. I am the owner and head of this school, but I have advisers, and those advisers slightly preferred Debbie. Only slightly; she has a beautiful body and excellent technique for her age. But you, to my mind, had something more and since then you have proved it. *I* gave you Betty, but this time everyone agreed.'

'*You* gave me Betty, Madame?' I wished I wasn't behaving like a parrot, but I had to say something.

She gave me a quick, bright glance, then shot at me:

'What did you call that dance you made up in the hall the other day?'

I gasped.

'But no one saw! I *know* there was no one there. You only came afterwards.'

'Child, I was up on the stage, looking at a rent in the curtain. They were slightly across the stage, you know. And so I watched you, and I was—more than interested. It was a good little dance and full of feeling.'

I said with difficulty, for I was so moved, so amazed:

'It—It was a Spring Dance. There were crocuses out in Bloomsbury Square and—and the sun was warm and I could smell spring coming.'

'Yes, and you interpreted it well. Now I'm glad we understand each other and you had better go back to your lessons now, and in future try and forget this inferiority complex over your sister.'

I rose. Was that *all* she was going to say?

'But, Madame, Betty—'

'What about Betty?'

'I—I thought—I was quite sure that you'd take her away from me.'

She cackled again.

'Wrong again, Doria Darke. You may keep Betty and mind you dance well. Off you go now.'

'Oh, *thank* you, Madame!' And then I fled. I raced up the stairs, quite forgetting my ankle.

I was going to dance on the Lingeraux stage! I was, perhaps for the first time for years, really sure of my own important identity. Doria Darke of the Lingeraux Ballet School.

14

The Princess in the Secret Wood

After that the last weeks of term simply flew. There were school examinations to occupy us, for one thing, and then, of course, there were rehearsals.

I loved *The Princess in the Secret Wood* from the start. The music was sometimes gay and sometimes almost eerie and I soon knew it off by heart. I had learned to whistle and I whistled those dances so endlessly that Aunt Eileen vowed that, if I didn't stop, she wouldn't come to see us dance. But, though I did try to stop, or at least to whistle something else, the others had caught it and could often be heard dashing up or downstairs whistling Betty's dance or bits from the rest of the ballet.

Debbie loved *Moon in a Net*, too. I think she particularly enjoyed rehearsing with the older ones, and Lotti and Claudia seemed to envy her.

Debbie and I had gone back to our old happier relationship. We had our ups and downs, of course, but now we could talk again nothing mattered very much. Whenever I was tempted to think that she was prettier, or cleverer, or a better dancer, I remembered some of the things Madame had said and at once felt better and more confident.

Spring had really come at last. There were daffodils out in the parks and delicate sprays of blossom. In St James's Park the willows were brilliantly green and all the other London trees were covered with a soft, shrill fuzz of bright buds.

Peter, Mel and I were very happy. We made a spendid trio, sometimes increased to a quartette by the presence of another boy called Denny Grenville, a small, cheerful Londoner who had been at the Lingeraux for just one term longer than we had. Sometimes Peter and I talked of the joys of being home at Easter, but I think he had quite settled down above the shop in St Pancras. His relatives were quite nice, though a bit rough and ready and not greatly in sympathy with a boy who wanted to be a ballet dancer. They would have understood it far better if he had wanted to be a professional footballer. All the same, his uncle and aunt had promised to come to the Spring Show.

Aunt Eileen would come, we knew, in spite of her remarks, and Linda had promised to be there, too. Clyde Smith took two tickets and said he was bringing Rachel. They were growing very friendly, which pleased me enormously, for I liked them both so much. I even hoped that their friendship would grow into something more. Rachel could probably be a scientist in America just as well, if not better, than in Britain.

The one thing that saddened Debbie and me a little was that Mother had written to say that she didn't think they could make the expensive journey south, though maybe they would another year. It would have made everything just perfect to have them there, but, in any case, we would be going home the very day after the Show. It was quite strange to think of seeing Birkenhead again and all our old friends. I longed to see Bunty and Bim, especially Bim, for three months can make such a difference to a little boy.

Easter was so late that the holidays were going to be unusually short, but we planned to make the best of the time at home.

Our costumes for the ballet were made in the Lingeraux workrooms, and we all had to go for fittings, which was very exciting. Debbie's moon dress was a silvery tunic, and she was to wear silver ballet shoes and a silver band on her hair. I, as Betty, was to wear a soft, short dress in a vivid rose pink. The other village girls were to be in yellow, blue or paler pink; Betty had to stand out.

The costumes were deliberately kept simple and as cheap as possible, but I was rather conscious that it was another expense. We didn't get them under our scholarships, but had to pay for them.

So the April days passed, the exams came and went and I hoped that I had done well. I was only really afraid of the maths papers, for figures were not my strong point. The ballets—our ballet, anyway—was almost ready and the dress rehearsal loomed ahead. I was thrilled, but, as the Show drew nearer, I was also nervous. For it would be terrible if I didn't dance well, after all. Madame Lingeraux had given me the part and she believed in me. I just had to justify her trust.

'I feel terrified, though,' I said to Mel, as we walked along Great Russell Street, just the two of us for once, on the afternoon before the dress rehearsal. 'Debbie's hardly ever nervous, but I always used to be before the Grayland shows, and they didn't matter nearly as much as this one.'

Mel nodded.

'I know. I'm almost glad now that I'm only a tree. We get some nice dances, anyway. Think if we ever become real dancers; we'll have to face it all the time, and critics as well.'

'Some ballerinas are always nervous before a performance, they say,' I remarked. 'They never grow out of it.'

All the same, though I was all fluttery with excitement and fright, the dress rehearsal went off well. It was glorious to be behind the scenes in the Lingeraux Theatre; it got into my blood and I knew that I was going to want it often. Though of course it might not happen again for years. Our ballet, that had started off as a series of apparently unconnected dances, seemed like a kind of miracle in its entirety, and the music sounded quite different when played by the

Lingeraux orchestra. Madame sat unnervingly in a box, and the principal ballet mistress sat out in front with most of the other ballet teachers. It was a relief when we could take our places in the circle and watch the other two ballets.

We broke up on the morning of the Spring Show and were then told to go home and rest. But 'resting' was just about the last thing we wanted to do, and Mel, Peter, Denny and I went to the Zoo. It was a curiously soothing place, especially watching the snakes, which always fascinated and slightly repelled me.

When I went home to tea I met Debbie in Gower Street; she had been out with Claudia and Lotti. Our tea was ready, but Aunt Eileen seemed a little remote and absent-minded. She wasn't very busy just then, because most of the students had gone home. Rachel had stayed for an extra night or two because of coming to the Show, and Clyde was off to spend Easter week-end with some American friends, leaving the next morning.

We had to be at the theatre early and Aunt Eileen seemed to be in a hurry to push us off.

'Get along, the pair of you. I have things to do. And stop looking so green, Dorrie; you'll be all right when the curtain goes up. What a child you are for showing emotion. Debbie is quite calm.'

Debbie grinned at her.

'I'm a bit fluttery, too, but I'm looking forward to it. You will come, Auntie? You and Linda?'

'Of course we'll come. It will be quite something for me to go anywhere with Linda. But it doesn't start until seven-thirty. I have to get into my best clothes before that.'

Her 'best clothes' were a dismal brown coat and a mud-coloured hat, once bought in a sale at Selfridge's. She had just no dress sense at all, but I felt very fond of her as she saw us off.

'You're sure you've got everything?'

'Everything, including our mascots,' Debbie assured her.

'Oh, those mascots! You ought to be ashamed of being so superstitious. What I say is—'

We didn't wait to hear her words of wisdom and she didn't seem to expect us to. We smiled and waved and set off through Bedford Square.

It was a dream of an evening, luminous and still, and I felt full of love for London, dear London. The high buildings shone in the lowering rays of the sun and the trees had that soft spring green that almost stops the heart. But then, when we reached the theatre, and walked in importantly at the stage door, I forgot everything but what was to come. I sniffed the stuffy, exciting atmosphere backstage and knew that it was my world, the world I wanted above all others.

Oh, it was so very thrilling, even though I was still terribly nervous. There was an air of controlled bustle, such as there might before a real professional performance. Electricians hurrying about, calling to each other, the Lingeraux stage manager in command.

Our ballet was first, then the junior one and finally *Moon in a Net*. So Debbie had to wait longer than me, but it had been decided that everyone was to get ready at once and then occupy themselves quietly in the dressing-rooms, taking turns to stand in the wings, if they were very quiet indeed. There were plenty of people in charge to see that we behaved. but Debbie was one who managed to slip on to the stage as the audience was arriving.

She came dashing back to me, where I was warming up with others in the first ballet. She looked most unusually startled; her eyes were big and full of news.

'Dorrie! Dorrie! I think I'm seeing things! Do come and look!'

'Everyone off stage in a few moments, except for the beginners in *The Princess*,' said Miss Verney, frowning at her.

'But please, Miss Verney, she *must* see! It's so extraordinary. Our father and mother are sitting in the third row, with Aunt Eileen and Linda, and they weren't coming. *We* didn't get the tickets.'

'They can't be!' I cried, and darted after her. 'They're two hundred miles away.'

The stage manager frowned at us from the prompt side, but we were already peering through the tiny gap in the curtains. Beyond was the lovely little red and gold auditorium, brilliantly lighted, and the seats were already almost full. It took me several moments to train my eyes on the middle of the third row, where—incredibly—sat Dad and Mother. Mother was reading the programme; I could just see her face. She was wearing a new hat, blue with a small blue flower. It gave me the most extraordinary feeling to see them there; real again at last. It was like a miracle, for we had been told so emphatically, three weeks earlier, that they wouldn't be coming. It explained Aunt Eileen's preoccupied air and the way she had wanted to get rid of us.

'Isn't it wonderful? *Now* we'll have to dance superbly,' Debbie cried.

Debbie was then swept away by the stage manager and I continued to warm up, my thoughts whirling. But I knew I only had to think of Betty, of the coming ballet, and I did my best to concentrate on the secret wood.

'Overture and beginners. . . .' We heard the music of the overture beyond the thick curtains. My mouth was dry and my knees felt weak. The village children opened the ballet.

And then the curtain rose, the auditorium was a dark blur, and we were dancing against our background of painted scenery. And suddenly I was no longer nervous, but very happy. I was Betty, a village child, surrounded by trees and meeting a Princess for the first time. I was frightened of the Green Witch . . . I was lost in the atmosphere of the ballet.

When my own little solo came part of my mind seemed to stand apart, as though I were someone

174

else, sitting out in the audience. And that other person could see the bright stage and the solitary, pink-clad figure that was me.

It was my night of nights ... my dream world come true, if only briefly in one little ballet. It seemed to be over so quickly; the curtain came swishing down and the applause rang out behind the heavy folds.

Then the curtain rose again for all the dancers to be seen, and after that Claudia, Caroline and Serge went out in front, to bow and smile and to have their extra rounds of applause. Then the Green Witch alone and finally me. Claudia and Caroline were presented with flowers, but I had not expected any. However, two bouquets were handed to me and I stood there in the blaze of light, blinking and almost overcome. Not important ... the real thing still unimaginably far away ... but then, just for those moments, it seemed real.

I found myself back in the wings, back in the dressing-room I was sharing with a number of others Debbie was there and took the flowers.

'I say! From Clyde and Rachel! And from Dad and Mother, Aunt Eileen and Linda. And a note from Mother. Can I read it?'

'Do,' I said. Somehow I couldn't see properly.

Mother's note said: 'We are here, after all, and will come round after the show. Best love.'

Debbie had her little triumph, too. I watched from the O.P. corner throughout *Moon in a Net*. She looked lovely in her silvery costume, with her flying silvery hair. A little New Moon, enchantingly fair. And Debbie had two bouquets as well and was starry-eyed with happiness.

'Oh, Dorrie,' she said, clutching her flowers, 'if this is what it feels like I'll work until I drop!'

They all came behind as they had promised. By then I was in my ordinary clothes and had taken off my make-up, but Debbie was still in her moon-tunic. Mother looked very slightly red-eyed, but said she had enjoyed every moment.

'I had to pinch myself to make myself believe you were my twins. Oh, Dorrie! Oh, Debbie!'

We hugged Dad and Mother unashamedly. No one was noticing, anyway. There was a terrific mob.

'But why did you come? It's wonderful, but we thought—'

'We changed our plans. Something came up. You'll hear in time. It's a secret and a surprise.'

'But Bunty and Bim?'

'Mrs Brown has taken them. We're all staying in London until the day after tomorrow.'

They would say no more, and neither would Aunt Eileen or Linda. We all went home in a taxi—great luxury—and there was a real new moon shining down over London. I couldn't imagine what the second surprise might be.

The Second Surprise

No one would tell us anything. That night we were
sent up to bed just as soon as we had had some milk
and biscuits. Mother came to see us in our garret
when we were in bed and I thought she looked round
critically, but she made no comment.

'We like it,' I said defensively. 'It was terribly
cold in the winter, in spite of the fire, but we've
grown very fond of it.'

Mother just said 'Hum!' and went to look out of
the window, drawing back the curtains to see the
moonlit, lamplit view.

'You both like London?' she asked, after a few
moments.

'We *love* it!' said Debbie. 'There's no place
like it.'

Mother laughed, then tucked us in and kissed us
as she used to do when we were little.

'Try to go to sleep at once. I know it has been a
very thrilling evening.'

'But we won't sleep unless we know about the
surprise,' I said coaxingly.

She just laughed and went away.

No one would tell us in the morning, either, but Aunt Eileen said we were all going out together. It all seemed extremely mysterious, but we obediently went upstairs to get ready. It wasn't like Aunt Eileen to take jaunts in the morning, but when we came down she was waiting with Dad and Mother. Mother looked pink and pretty, and Dad looked rather handsome, too.

'And you won't tell us where we're going?' I asked, and they all laughed and shook their heads.

Well, it was really rather nice to have a surprise coming, for otherwise it might have been rather an anti-climax, with the Spring Show over for a whole year. By then I was familiar with many parts of London, for we had wandered quite widely during the past weeks, and also I never ceased to enjoy my London street map. But in any case we didn't go far, though we travelled on three buses. The third bus we took for just a few stops down Vauxhall Bridge Road. Debbie kept catching my eye and once she shook her head. It was all very strange, but interesting, even exciting. We sensed that the three adults were also rather excited, even Aunt Eileen.

Vauxhall Bridge Road is by no means beautiful, but after we left the bus we soon turned off it, heading towards the south end of Vincent Square, which is a simply huge green stretch given over to the playing-fields of Westminster School. I named it before we quite got there and Aunt Eileen said:

'She's a real Londoner already.'

We were soon in a quiet, old-fashioned street. It had a few shops and some rows of small, ordinary houses, fronting straight on to the pavement.

'Between here and the Tate there are mostly new blocks of flats,' Aunt Eileen remarked.

'Are we going to the Tate Gallery then?' Debbie demanded. But Aunt Eileen had stopped outside one of the houses and was taking a key from her purse. I noticed then that the house was empty. It was quite newly painted, with a yellow front door.

Aunt Eileen opened the door, and, silent and puzzled, Debbie and I followed them into a small, cream-painted hall. All the doors were open, showing empty rooms, very scrubbed and clean.

'But why have we come?' Debbie asked, standing on one foot and staring into the neat little kitchen. It was modern, though the house must be quite old. 'Whose house is it? Why—?'

'All in good time,' said Aunt Eileen and began to show the house to Dad and Mother. They went from room to room, exclaiming over cupboard space and electric light fittings, the number and size of the bedrooms. Debbie and I trailed behind, grimacing at each other.

'It's really rather nice,' Mother was saying. 'Quite a big yard, almost a garden, with that flower-bed and the plane tree. And it isn't far from the bus.'

'Is Aunt Eileen going to move here, do you think?' Debbie hissed at me.

179

A wild suspicion was starting in my mind, but I couldn't really believe it.

'Do you think *we* are?' I hissed back, and she looked startled, tossing back her hair.

'How could we? Dad works in Birkenhead.'

'Just for the next two weeks,' Dad said suddenly. 'After that I shall be working in London.'

We shrieked and the sound echoed through the empty house.

'But how . . . why? You can't mean it! You mean we'll live with you and not in Gower Street? That—'

'I believe they'll miss your house,' Mother said, laughing. 'Oh, we came up quite early yesterday and your dad had an interview. He got the job and is to start in two weeks' time, so we shall have to buckle to when we get home. There'll be a lot to do. He will be working in the radio and television department of one of the big stores. Not as manager—just yet, anyway—but the money is more than he's getting now. And your aunt had promised that, if he got the job, she could find us a house. It belongs to her husband's brother, who owns quite a lot of property in these parts and he's willing to rent it to us. Otherwise we'd hardly have managed, as houses or flats are so difficult to get in London.'

'We hope you're pleased,' Dad said, and we both hugged him at once and talked loudly, trying to drown each other.

Then we looked at the house more carefully, since

it was going to be home. It was certainly small, perhaps too small for six of us, but I thought how glorious it was going to be to be so near the Tate and the river.

'But I hope you'll often come and see me,' Aunt Eileen said, as we walked back to the bus stop. 'I shall miss the pair of you.' She even looked quite fondly at Debbie, and Debbie actually blushed.

'Oh, of *course* we will,' I promised. 'We'll miss you, too, and all the students and dear, dear Ruari.'

I felt just a little sad as we went back to Gower Street for lunch. It would be wonderful to have Dad and Mother, Bunty and Bim in London, and not far away; to go home every evening from the Lingeraux and to be able to see Mel in the holidays as well as in term-time. Yet I should miss our strangely romantic garret in Gower Street and all the excitements of the students' lives.

'I shall miss it, too,' Debbie agreed, when we were back in the garret. She turned a couple of pirouettes, then took my hand. We danced a wild *pas de deux*, leaping and twirling in what space there was.

'The Darke dancers!' Debbie gasped, just as the door opened and Aunt Eileen came in.

'Good heavens, girls! You'll have the ceiling down in the room below. This is no place for your capers. Lunch is ready.'

We followed her meekly down the stairs; those

familiar stairs that had seen so much of my suffering. Our first term at ballet school was over, but next term we would dance again in Bloomsbury Square.